ALSO BY

CAROLE MARTINEZ

The Threads of the Heart

THE CASTLE
OF WHISPERS

Carole Martinez

THE CASTLE OF WHISPERS

*Translated from the French
by Howard Curtis*

Europa
editions

Europa Editions
214 West 29th Street
New York, N.Y. 10001
www.europaeditions.com
info@europaeditions.com

Copyright © 2011 by Editions Gallimard, Paris
First Publication 2014 by Europa Editions

Translation by Howard Curtis
Original title: *Du domaine des murmures*
Translation copyright © 2014 by Europa Editions

Library of Congress Cataloging in Publication Data is available
ISBN 978-1-60945-182-0

Martinez, Carole
The Castle of Whispers

Book design and cover illustration by Emanuele Ragnisco
www.mekkanografici.com

Prepress by Grafica Punto Print – Rome

Printed in the USA

*To Richard, Marie-Noëlle and Renaud Martinez,
my parents and my brother, with all my love.*

To Frasquita Carasco.

Of the ladies of the twelfth century,
I shall therefore once again capture only an image.
A mere reflection, flickering and distorted.
—GEORGES DUBY

THE CASTLE
OF WHISPERS

PROLOGUE

The Castle of Whispers can be reached from the north, although only those who know the area would venture on the path that cuts through the thick forest from the Meadow of the Green Lady. This scar between the trees has been maintained by generations of men who have lopped off the branches as they grew back, struggling ceaselessly to stop the woods from closing over it again.

The almost faded path, on which we walk for a long time, echoes to the cries of birds. We proceed with difficulty, having to press down with our toes to free our feet from the muddy soil, the earth gradually sloping upwards. Brambles clutch at our ankles and scratch our faces, and little brown spiders run over the moss between the leaves. We advance beneath the vault of trees, lighted only by rare shafts of sun that streak the undergrowth with gold, like the illuminations in an old book of fairy tales.

At last the foliage opens and we come out into a large clearing, once encircled by a gigantic fence of dead trunks and then, two centuries later, by a wall of rubble stones so high that the top of the great tower beyond it was barely visible. Today, all that remain of those ramparts are a few ruins of the old curtain walls that surrounded on three sides the dazzling gap where the Castle of Whispers rises.

On the south side, there was no need for walls, whether of wood or stone: the seigniorial tower spread its incomplete wings atop a cliff plunging straight down to the River Loue.

The tranquil river still laps at the rocky escarpment, making every effort, as it has always done, to draw the same green loops across the land.

Defying the void, the castle towers over a horizon black with forest.

It has grown from the soil in successive bursts, rising—or, rather, spreading—in the course of time. Each of its masters has left his mark on it, one adding a stretch of wall, another a flight of stairs, yet another a turret, taking no heed of the unity of the whole.

We pass the spot where the huge gate of oak and iron once stood, and tread the tall grass of the fallow grounds that stretch before the north face of the castle.

A light breeze caresses our faces, ruffles our hair, makes us screw up our eyes, tickles the insides of our ears. The sound of the wind bends the wild grass, as if a dress with a long train has passed over it. The wind is whispering something, a distant sorrow, as it frays in the air.

We advance into the wind, surrounded by that long whisper that seems to escape from the stones.

And the route we have taken to get here, that forest, those deep woods, that odor of humus, that river with its green curves that we know is below: all that is hidden and seems unreal. The whole fortress sways before our eyes. For this castle is built not only of white stones piled neatly one on top of the other, or even of words written somewhere in a book, or of flying leaves scattered here and there like seeds, this castle is not built of lines declaimed on a stage by an actor using his fine, firm voice and his whole body like an ivory instrument.

No, this place is woven from whispers, from the intermingling of thin voices so old that we must listen carefully to be aware of them. Words never written down, but knotted together and drawn out in a soft hiss.

A tiny breath rises over the blank page, threads its way between the stones, stirs our souls, and it is in this breath that we make out the vibrant shadow of a castle like those we built when we were children. And this ghostly shrine devours the majestic monument that stood before us, solid and historic, only a few seconds ago. The whispers draw fleeting shadows on its austere façade, and we wait with hearts pounding, we wait to see things more clearly.

The seigniorial tower becomes blurred with a host of whispers, the mineral screen cracks, the page darkens, opens dizzyingly on a swarming afterlife, and we agree to fall into the abyss, in order to draw from it the liquid voices of forgotten women oozing around us.

I am a talking shadow.
I am she who went into voluntary reclusion in an attempt to live.
I am the Virgin of the Whispers.

To you who can hear, I want to be the first to speak, to tell of my century, to tell of my dreams, to tell of the hopes of the walled-up women.

In this year 1187, Esclarmonde, Damsel of the Whispers, resolves to live as an anchoress at Hautepierre, confined until her death to the little sealed cell built for her by her father against the walls of the chapel that he erected on his lands in honor of Saint Agnes, who was martyred at the age of thirteen for having accepted no other bridegroom than Christ.

I tried to acquire spiritual strength, I dreamed of being no more than a prayer and of observing my time through a spy-hole, a barred opening through which, for years, my food was passed to me. This stone mouth became mine, my only orifice. Because of it, I was able to speak at last, to whisper in the ears of men and urge them to do what my lips could never have obtained, even with the sweetest of kisses.

My stone mouth gave me the power of a saint. I breathed my will through that little window, and my breath traveled through the world as far as the gates of Jerusalem. From their half-open tomb, my eyes followed the Crusaders on their journey toward Acre, formerly Ptolemais.

But my voice was not liked, and it was torn from me. And the swallowed sentences, the stillborn words are choking me. A host of subterranean sorrows torment me. What has not been said swells my soul, a coagulated stream, boils of silence to be lanced, from which will flow the river of pus that keeps me between these stones, that long ribbon of black water bearing the carcasses of emotions, drowned cries, their bellies swollen with night, abortive words of love. Words that will bleed and then lie petrified in the mud.

Come into the dark water, drown in my tales, let my words lead you down paths and gullies that no living soul has yet taken.

I want to speak until I can no longer breathe.

Listen!

I am Esclarmonde, the sacrificial victim, the dove, the flesh offered to God, His share.

You have no idea how beautiful I was, as beautiful as a girl can be at the age of fifteen, so beautiful and fine that my father never tired of gazing at me and could not make up his mind to yield me to another. I had inherited my mother's exceptionally luminous skin. Behind my alabaster face and unusually clear eyes, an elusive flame seemed to flicker.

But the neighboring lords lay in wait for their prey.

I was the only daughter and I would have a fine dowry.

Surrounded by the vigorous sons God had given my father, as well as his companions at arms and their young squires, I was a bird, and I sang constantly, I sang what modesty forbade me to say amid the clangor of hooves and arms. I echoed like a glass bell in the middle of the enclosed garden where I was kept in fine weather, part of a millefleur tapestry along with the wild buttercups and gladioli torn from the meadows of the countryside, and from out of their mingled scents my voice rose toward God, light and clear, my voice rose like the smoke of Abel.

Everyone in the region spoke of the damsel, the sweet angel, so well guarded within the Whispers, standing there on the fresh lawn of its high meadow, and it was said that in order to reach that castle on the edge of a cliff all one had to do was follow that ever-clear voice through the forest, a voice that only night seemed able to extinguish.

I had been designed and molded by the words of men. All of us women were, in that time and place, but my father no doubt was a better sculptor, he had forgotten to talk to me about the faults of my sex, and had thrown out his chaplain, who could not keep silent! Imagine how they must all have dreamed of that sweet, well-behaved damsel, that guiding song of a virgin, that treasure attached to my name, that child so loved by her father!

But nobody cared about my desires.

Who would have wandered so far astray as to question a young woman, even a princess, about her wishes?

In those days, a woman's words were nothing but idle chatter, a woman's desires dangerous whims, to be dismissed with a word, or a blow of the birch.

My father, though, was gentle with me among the men of war. The only thing he obstinately opposed was the idea of sending me where God demanded me. He rejected the convent, which would have torn me from him more surely than any marriage.

He was a minor lord but a great knight, and he had carved out such a fine reputation for himself, both at tournaments and in battle, that many were the boys he must have trained: my maternal cousins, the eldest sons of his vassals, some younger sons of more powerful lords. Our world overflowed with horses and dogs and young men speaking loudly, drinking, hunting and following me with their eyes.

Of all those our father welcomed into our home, the one he loved the most was Lothaire, youngest son of the Lord of Montfaucon. This powerful neighbor had entrusted his boy to my father at the age of eight, before dubbing him a knight.

After his dubbing, Lothaire had competed in tournaments, throwing himself fiercely into the fray, fearing neither his adversaries nor the demons one sometimes saw fluttering over the fields and lists and carrying away the souls of the dead—

for whoever died in such contests, then forbidden by the Church, was not entitled to a Christian burial. For two fine seasons he had gone from place to place in search of prestige, selling off the arms and chargers he had won during these confrontations in order to celebrate his exploits worthily, living in grand style, courted by very important persons wishing to include him in their bands of knights. For two fine seasons he had been honored in this way, before stopping in his tracks and returning home.

He returned to me all wreathed in victories but, in my eyes, his face had kept its plumpness, and all I could see in him was a capricious child in a metal suit, trained to kill, always in chain mail and on horseback, dismounting only to tumble the peasant girls whenever the desire took him. I knew how badly he behaved from those daughters of serfs who came to the castle to sew and weave as part of their bonded labor. Of all of them, they said, this boy with his fine slate-gray eyes was the greediest for caresses, the one who most loved to plunder the virtues of women. Never asking anything, never even waiting for an inviting glance, he used his member as if it were a sword! And the girls who had been deflowered said nothing, to avoid ignominy, to avoid being thrown out on the roads.

My age loved virgins. I knew that I had to protect myself, to protect my true treasure, my father's honor, that untouched seal that was supposed to open the kingdom of Heaven to me.

And it was this man, this Lothaire de Montfaucon, who drew me into the game of courtly love, because that was what he wanted. Attempting to civilize his desire, he would go down on one knee and implore me to grant him a kiss. All those stories of brave knights in the service of their ladies did not interest me! Other girls doubtless longed for troubadours and delighted in songs of love, in the lady's capitulation after a long siege, wondering anxiously if the champion would take his lady love. But I had ceased to tremble for these young men-at-arms, for I had realized that the beauty always succumbed in such tales, the knight won all his battles. How could one doubt his power? The struggle was an unequal one, lost in advance. The lady had to accept the homage. She would put him to the test, of course, but once he had overcome all the obstacles she would offer herself as a reward to him, for being patient and not simply unlacing his britches. These stories were all in praise of him, the only true victor of the game of love. Merely taking the woman they wanted had no doubt become too easy for these violent men, and so they had invented this refinement.

I would never have wanted that boy. I felt only disgust for him. He might be all grace and elegance with me, but as far as I was concerned he was ugly inside. And I did not accept the idea of changing hands.

But now my father had yielded, and Lothaire and I had been made to get up on a fine marriage chest, where he had taken my trembling little hand in his big hand. We were now betrothed to one another, and my fiancé paid court to me in the manner of the century. He loved himself passionately in that role, which, for someone who had never been able to wait, was a new and difficult one. It was expected of me that I follow the rules, that I subjugate his desire for however long the betrothal lasted, that I resist valiantly. As I had been taught, I neither looked at him nor spoke when, with my father's consent, he would come into the ladies' chamber on his return from the hunt to tell us of his exploits. But in spite of myself, I could not close my ears to the awful verbiage of the man who would soon be my master—of that he had no doubt.

Marriage was not to be taken lightly. I had no choice, any more than did Lothaire, for the Church demanded only that both families agree. But Lothaire stood to gain a great deal: as the youngest in his great house, he had little chance of escaping celibacy and the wandering of the paladin. The eldest had had their share, and the names of the two youngest were not expected to pass into posterity. Amey, five years his senior, having just missed a good match, had already renounced the idea of taking a wife. There remained Lothaire, gorged with rage and ambition.

His fiery spirit and his skill at tournaments had so distinguished him that, in everyone's opinion, even my father's, his manly blood deserved to be perpetuated. That made our union a godsend. Once married, he would become a lord in his turn: his wife, however frail, docile, and silent, would give him the substance he needed by making him the founder of a line. There were still places to be taken in the earldom of Burgundy. My womb would project him into the future. He would till my flesh as he wished so that his glory could take root in it, so that his descendants could become a forest, fine boys who would bear his name when he was gone, who would harbor his blood, his memory, his fame for centuries to come—not to mention the dowry and the alliance attached to the woman who was being given to him until death do them part.

I would be nothing but a modest container whom successive pregnancies would finally carry away. And even if Lothaire died before me, my widowhood would not protect me, but would abandon me again to the highest bidder as a token of some alliance or other.

How could I escape this fate except with the help of Christ?

Christ was powerful in the minds of the women of my time. Christ alone could keep men in check and rescue a virgin from their grasp. Families believed that in giving up their child to God they were sealing a new alliance with Heaven, for that child would pray for them from the summit of the skies or the cell of a cloister.

This force of prayer, this spiritual energy, held the balance of the world. Nobody doubted that at the time.

Beguines, mystics, voluntary anchoresses, all sometimes managed to lead their entourage and gain a freedom that was otherwise inconceivable. It was an autonomy to which almost no other woman of my class could lay claim.

But at what price?

I would so have liked not to displease my father.

One morning in May, I was awakened before dawn to be dressed and adorned, then taken, stiff with fabrics and anguish, to Montfaucon. Sumptuously harnessed and covered with little silver bells, the finest horses of the Whispers bore my litter, and all the household went with me. It was a great procession, filled with gaudy banners and the irritating jingling of the bells. All that merrymaking around my small person: doubtless they were trying to make me look bigger by surrounding me with all this commotion!

My father strutted on his palfrey, displaying his treasure for the last time. I was the honor of his blood.

The sky rumbled, thick with clouds. The light was almost yellow, and increasingly strange. Thunder rolled in the valley, echoed behind us, galloped beneath my ribs. As we advanced, I waited for the rain to come and wash away my fear, but the storm remained a dry one, and only the lightning streaked my slate-gray horizon.

The clouds broke all at once, and rain came crashing down like a portcullis onto the square in front of the church of the Franches Montagnes, where the wedding party had taken shelter. Loudly though the church's two bells pealed, they were unable to drown out the storm. In order not to ruin my robe, I was forced to pass through that curtain of water beneath my father's cape.

My betrothed was waiting for me in his gleaming costume. It was raining so hard that we would exchange vows, not in the open air as custom dictated, but in the nave.

There, facing the archbishop clad in his pallium—he had come in person to marry his nephew to the daughter of one of his vassals—I did not say yes.

Never had a local girl dared such an affront.

Then, knowing that such an act would never be forgiven, I took out the little knife I had been hiding beneath my ceremonial dress and, taking as my model Ode, who would later be a saint, I cut off my ear. Addressing the archbishop, I declared that I had offered myself to Christ, but that nobody thus far had wanted to hear it, so hard is it for a girl to be listened to even by a fair and loving father.

I had resolved to cut off my nose, but I must have had pity on my beauty and decided to spare my face and remove just that one ear. The cartilage had resisted my blade somewhat, even though I had carefully sharpened it.

Once over their initial shock, the wedding party grew silent at the sight of my blood and listened to my voice. The breath that carried my words was not a natural one. The power of my commitment, Lothaire's calm demeanor—though publicly rejected by a girl of fifteen, he did not protest but stood frozen by my side, as if seeing me for the first time— the way I withstood the pain, my statuesque beauty, and that long ribbon of blood in my golden tresses, in my transparent veil: everything suddenly seemed to them a miracle.

Added to that was the liquid sky surrounding the scene, the screaming of the wind-lashed trees, and the surprising immobility of the great pontiff in his purple robe, crozier in his hand. The storm was spitting its rage, rumbling like a huge beast, as I calmly said no to Archbishop Thierry II, vicar of Christ and my father's feudal lord, and to my father, and to Lothaire, and to my masters present and to come. For the first time in my life I said no.

I added that Christ wished my dowry to be used to erect a stone chapel at the Whispers and for a cell to be built for me against its walls, where I would be confined forever. God had other plans for me than marriage to Lothaire. Once built, the chapel would be dedicated to Saint Agnes, and from my tomb, at once living and dead, I would pray for all those I had offended by my rejection.

It was then that the lamb entered the church.

It advanced through the crowd, frail on its long, quivering legs, and trotted toward me. In the silence that had fallen, its shrill bleating came to magnify my gesture and seal the agreement of Heaven, and nobody dreamed of calling me a heretic!

Thanks to that apparition, I was a new Agnes who would only have to sacrifice one ear.

The scene caused a great stir in the region. The archbishop intervened: deeply impressed, he talked of a miracle, and managed to calm the rage of the lord of Montfaucon, his brother.

Like Lothaire, my father did not say a word.

I t was only on the evening of my abortive wedding that my
father cried out.

We had all returned to the castle, our wedding garments
muddy and engorged with rain. My long sky-blue pelisse with
its sable lining was such a burden to me that, exhausted as I
was by the journey, I could barely stand it—it took several days
to get dry. The castle's maidservants took an eternity to strip
me, to extricate me from all the layers of soaking cloth in which
I had been bound that very morning and which now clung to
my body. Once liberated, freed of all that fabric, I was wiped
down, my ear was bandaged, and then I was laid in my bed
beside my old aunt, who was weeping to see her lineage tarnished by my sin. But I was already asleep standing up, I had
been sleeping since the middle of the journey, I had slept during the ride through the storm, I had dreamed that mad, head-
long return. Cradled by the breath of the maidservants dozing
on the floor of the ladies' chamber, curled up against the naked
body of my aunt with her ice-cold feet, I was suddenly awakened by my father's long pitiful cry, and I was aware of his
thoughts in that one cry, I read into his soul.

It seemed to me that God had made me porous, that he had
opened my father's mind to me, as he would subsequently
open the minds of so many others.

I knew then all that my father's silence had hidden from me.

I had chosen to die to the world at the age of fifteen, and
had drained myself of his blood in front of everyone. He had

no desire to seal a new alliance with God. He had already given up a son to him, Benoît, eight years my senior, who had preferred prayer to arms, had been trained at Saint-Jean, and had for the past year been directing the little priory at Hautepierre, barely one league from the castle. God was insatiable: He had also stolen from him his wife and five of the children she had borne him. But that was not enough. Now this unappeasable God had taken his only daughter.

His cry, I realized, was filled with a sense of powerlessness.

The thread of his thought continued to unreel in my mind that night, as if it had been uttered aloud and addressed directly to me.

If God was demanding his only daughter alive, it was doubtless to punish him for having loved her too much, guarded her too closely, looked at her too long. There seemed to have been something guilty about his love for his child. What kind of father was he to feel this separation so violently? Fathers never felt such things. The unreasoning love of children was a matter for women. Men turned away from them, especially from their daughters, who lived in another sphere, a feminine sphere, with its mystery, its weakness, its wretched imperfection. Men were supposed to love in a better way, without excess, without softness. They took care of their offspring at a distance and their word was like the blade of a sword.

My father, though, had taken so much pleasure in pampering me, coming into the ladies' chamber to be deloused, devoting more time to me than he should have, teaching me about horses and falcons, teaching me as much as he taught his sons—perhaps even more, since each of them had left him at the age of seven to train with other lords, or to live either with families allied with ours or among the monks. He had initiated me into all that, while keeping me in a cage. I was his wonderful lark with clipped wings. Only my falcon made light of the wooden ramparts that blocked the forest from me. Sometimes it dragged me with it in its flight. Together, we circled high in the sky.

I had shared my father's life for fifteen years, and he had never lived with anyone so long—neither with his mother, a gentle presence lost at the age when boys became pages, nor even with his wife, who had died giving birth to his eighth son. That adoring gaze I had always turned on him had made him a better man. He would miss that gaze so much!

But by shedding his blood in church I had denied it, and had chosen for myself a master against whom nobody could fight. I was leaving him, abandoning him to himself. I preferred God, that devourer of lives. Between the Heavenly Father and my physical father, I had chosen to glorify the former at the expense of the latter. It had been a terrible humiliation. By rebelling in front of everyone, I had betrayed him, soiled him, dishonored him.

His love for me had been a mistake, he thought. It had made him soft, and his authority had suffered because of it. He blamed my betrayal for the pain that pierced his belly.

That blood on the veil around my hair, that blood on my cheek and my braids and my mantle, heavy with embroidery and all the women's hands that had worked on it for weeks—that blood was his. I owed it to him, and I had chosen to shed it.

Let the ungrateful child who spilled her father's blood on her wedding day disappear into the tomb!

He would give this stranger the robe of stone that she demanded and allow her to join her heavenly bridegroom. And then he would leave her in her nuptial tomb and forget her!

His widowhood had lasted all too long. He would take a new wife. Seven years had passed without it even crossing his mind, though there was no shortage of marriageable girls in the earldom, excellent matches that would have reinforced his power. A stepmother would have found the words to bring this stubborn girl to heel! How stupid not to have imposed one on his unruly child for fear of upsetting her! And what a terrible thing it was to see that beautiful face amputated!

He had not found any trace of the fallen ear on the flagstones of the deserted church. He had searched for that fragment of his daughter, that appendage that I had cut off with a steady hand. My gesture had been such a surprise, it had cut short his anger as a father, his anger as a lord, his anger as a warrior—that anger had fallen along with his mutilated daughter's flesh. Through the force of a small, sharp woman's knife, his anger had joined my ear on the floor of the nave. It had rolled into a corner of the church, and he had fallen silent, as though gagged by the calm certainty of my words. Remaining alone on the scene after the scandal, after the miracle of the lamb, he had found nothing but that anger. As for my ear, it had disappeared. The double doors of the church stood wide open on the curtain of rain, behind which he had withdrawn, hiding his shame. Everyone else was gone, the wedding party was ruined, even the poor had not waited for the traditional distribution of alms.

From that point on, he hated his daughter as much as he hated God.

It was that twofold hatred he was screaming now into the night. And I felt horribly upset with myself for having made my father such an enemy of the Almighty. I was so afraid that his anger would lead him straight to Hell, that he would oppose my destiny and make beatitude impossible for both of us.

Father did not speak to me for months, but he obeyed and had a chapel built in the precinct of the Whispers, using all the resources of his fiefdom to erect its smooth walls: the ardor and faith of his people, and the good stones from his quarry on the banks of the river below the castle. Several generations of quarriers had already come and gone, extracting the white substance of the castle from the cliff. It was time for my father to take his place in the line of builder-lords and use the same wild rock his grandfather, Achard, had used to build the great tower of the castle and replace its wooden ancestor. High up there on its rocky spur overhanging the valley of the Loue, all adorned with banners, it had initially been seen as a challenge to God. Achard's heir was called Guillaume. Having so often seen his father struggling with stones, he had acquired a taste for the same fight, so much so that he had devoted part of his life to a new construction project: to erect a permanent seigniorial dwelling on the edge of the precipice. He himself had designed the imposing building adjoining the tower—that eastern flank of the Whispers where nobody goes any longer now that the centuries have passed, but which in its time was something of a wonder. He had drawn an outline of the *aula* on the ground with the help of his twelve-knotted rope, then recruited a small army of stonecutters, masons, carpenters, and wood carvers to build his dream on its rocky ridge.

His eldest son, my father, spent his entire childhood walking in his footsteps, watching his men mix mortar, cut stones, or fell oaks, and had learned how to handle a plumb line before he could even hold a sword. And yet he took no part in this new project I had forced on him, instead hiring an itinerant foreman to supervise the work.

We lived for two years with the noise of cutting tools and hammers, two years during which I followed the construction of my little chapel with passionate interest. Each oak from which the ceiling beams would be taken was carefully chosen, each stone was shaped to fit in its rightful place, each nail held the structure together, and each of the bars of my window was forged before my eyes.

Only the bell was cast in the village.

How mild it was on the morning of my death!

Before sunrise, I had left the bed I still shared with my mad old aunt, donned a shift and my soft shoes, stepped over my foster sister Jehanne, and advanced between the other girls of the castle, who lay on the ground on their straw mattresses, forming a labyrinth of flesh as far as the door of the chamber. I carefully made my way in the darkness among their exhausted, almost motionless bodies. Ever since the inner ladders had been replaced by wooden steps, the women had taken the highest room in the tower.

I slipped almost naked into the night as if into a new robe.

It was a dawn on the verge of summer.

Sitting on the edge of the opening in the wall, on the stone shaped like a half moon that even now overlooks the abyss behind the Castle of Whispers, I gazed at the vast forest below. The great clearances of my century had not yet reduced it, and the horizon was a mass of undulant hills bristling with trees. I let myself be absorbed by that space still under the spell of night, a space I had seen for years from the window of my bed-chamber without ever being allowed to go out into it alone, free, to face the wind. It was that powerful landscape with which I wished to fill my tomb. The Whispers had been built on the edge of the void. On one side, the courtyard, the gardens, the thick wooden fence, and the steep slope kept the forest at bay. On the other, the building overhung a fantastic landscape, reigning like a lighthouse on its rock, suspended above an ocean of wood and the River Loue patiently lapping the cliff.

I had no doubts, I felt no fear, just a touch of nostalgia, a twinge beneath my ribs. God would be with me to push back the walls of my cell, God would give me even broader visions than this. I would contemplate His universe, I would travel within my stone recess.

I had chosen.

Five months earlier, Jehanne, who loved me, had asked to be confined with me, but I had refused.

"You will be more useful outside, and I've seen how the foreman's son has been making eyes at you."

"He wants me to follow him, to set off on the roads with him. But I'm dependent on this fiefdom. He forgets that my lord would pursue me, that he has rights over me and my off-spring, that the daughter of a serf doesn't belong to herself, and that any children we have together would inherit my con-dition. It isn't feet we peasants have, it's roots. It's not certain that anyone of my line could live elsewhere than on these lands."

"If your handsome sweetheart weds you, my father and his lands will let you leave. I am certain of it. Stop torturing your-self—you are not a tree, you will survive that exile!"

"And you, what would you do without a Jehanne to find you a lamb to leave bleating among the crowd at your wed-ding? What will you do without me when you are walled up? Who will take care of you in your desert?"

"God will provide. It was He who inspired you when you released that lamb, it was He who pushed the animal toward me. Leave, my dear! The man who helped to build Sainte-Agnès, the man who has been carving its stones with so much talent for nearly two years, deserves to have you with him."

"You know, the only time I've traveled was that time they

wanted to marry you and the whole household went with you to Montfaucon. For me, the world stops at the crossroads where the great crucifix stands. Beyond it, nobody knows my father's name. Beyond it, I wouldn't be Jehanne anymore, I'd be just a stranger tramping the roads, a vagabond. If I left here, I'd never be able to retrace my steps. Here, the smallest shrub is familiar to me—somebody from our house must have planted it or seen it grow. Nothing belongs to me, but I belong to these lands, and leaving them would be like falling into the void from the cliff of Hautepierre, or throwing myself into the Loue. Wherever I went, I wouldn't even be understood, because people speak differently. I'd have to walk in Pierre's footsteps and live with the fear of losing sight of him at every bend in the road. I'm not as brave as that!"

"I am even less brave than you! And I envy you for having run freely over my father's lands. We are browbeaten by rules and stories to keep us in our places, even though the world is the same beyond the great crucifix. Have no fear, the horizon conceals no demons. Might I, too, have left if I had not been so well guarded since I was a child? I found a little space only in the flight of my falcon and in prayer, and the one path our age offers me is an inner path. I have looked deeply into my faith in order to escape, and I know now that my only escape lies in being walled up. Isn't that remarkable?"

"But there'll hardly be any room for you to lie down in your cell!"

"I shan't be sleeping much."

Jehanne had wept, and I had dried her tears and told her about how crestfallen Lothaire had been during our last interview, how he had tried to steal a kiss, and how I had managed to keep him at a distance with a look. I had never had such power before. Henceforth, I could tame wild beasts! She had smiled, imagining the young man's embarrassment at his own rejection—he who only a few months earlier had blustered and considered himself a master.

We had decided that day that she would be present at my entombment, that she would marry outside my chapel then leave the fiefdom with her handsome stonecutter at her side and go to Paris, where a cathedral was thrusting upwards into the sky.

I had chosen, but separating myself from the world cost me more than I would have thought.

I had left my observation post as the first light of dawn was breaking, but I could not interrupt my last escapade so soon. Intoxicated with the fresh air, I untied the ribbon that held my hair in place and savored a few more minutes of freedom. Surrounded by the cries of birds, I walked along the precipice as far as the fence that protected the castle, its wooden out-buildings, its stables, and my chapel, the outline of which could at last be distinguished, freed of its scaffolding. Listening carefully, it was possible to hear the snoring of drunken men. The great hall was so crowded that some of my father's vassals had chosen to sleep outside. The peace that we had been enjoying for some months in the region had lulled the sentries into such a deep sense of security that no guard saw me lift the bar on the postern. Emboldened by this, I actually slipped outside the walls, my hair blowing in the wind, and took a few steps down the path that continued along the edge of the abyss as far as the limestone rock used as a hoist.

I wanted to fully enjoy that last dawn.

From the forest there rose a mist that shrouded it even more as it emerged from the darkness. I no longer feared anything, not even the inhabitants of the night, those creatures the old people would say only came out at night to avoid the gaze of God. With my fingers, I stroked the long red velvet ribbon embroidered with my name. The coolness of the woods licked my face, my damp shift stuck to my body, and I realized that I was shivering.

It was then that I heard him running after me. I barely had time to turn before his hand was crushing my mouth. His palm was salty. He pinned me to the ground amid the bracken, lifted my shift up to my chin, slipped his knees between my thighs, and forced them apart. I was caught in a vise between the loose earth and this heavy body crushing me, I felt his member tearing me apart as I struggled to breathe through my nose and he spat his own terrible breath in my face. I did not cry out when he freed my mouth, the better to grip me, the deeper to penetrate me. I had stopped struggling, having nothing more to protect now but my secret. He moved above me, moaning like a demon, pounding me as hard as he could with his member to reach his climax. He smelled of wine and war. His face twisted by a wicked smile, he emptied his bitterness and rage into me, then stood up again and disappeared into the mist.

The red ribbon where my Christian name was embroidered remained in the bracken.

Hiding the soiled hem of my shift and taking care not to meet anyone, I hurriedly retraced my steps all the way back to my chamber. By the time I reached it, Jehanne had just awakened. In the half light, nobody saw my earth-spattered face. I dismissed the other maidservants, as well as my old aunt Gertrude, who could only obey, and asked Jehanne to listen to me carefully and above all to keep silent about what I was telling her. I did not want what had just been stolen from me to stop me from entering my cell. Girls who had been forced lost their honor, so it was better to conceal such atrocities. In everyone's eyes, I would remain a virgin! Nuns sent by the archbishop had determined my virginity just two days previously. I would tell no one of my rape. The Devil would not gain anything from having profaned me thus! Jehanne understood: any woman, whether lady or servant, preferred silence to what our age considered shame.

Semen and blood were dripping down my bruised thighs—
that pink spring weeping between my legs reminded me of my
lost ribbon—and in my belly the Devil's thrusts still echoed.

Jehanne was already preparing the basin, the maids were
heating water and bricks for me to take a hot bath, and the
manservants were bringing up the buckets.

I slipped into the hot water like one attempting to forget.
Rose petals and rosemary leaves floated around my wounded
body. I had wanted to bathe as quickly as possible to wash
away the blood, to wipe out the outrage. I wanted my flesh to
have the complexion of a beautiful bride when she joined her
mystical bridegroom. As Jehanne rubbed my shoulders with
herbs, it occurred to me that I would soon be entering another
bath, a bath of prayers and tears, whose fecund waters would
purify me from within, scraping away the rust of sin until they
rendered my soul transparent. My hair was combed and tied—
a single lace in the middle of my back—to signify that I was no
longer free, my teeth were rubbed, and my mouth was washed
of the acrid taste that the Devil's hand had left there. Then
Jehanne, seeing me dressed and ready to leave, threw herself
into my arms one last time and sobbed. We were the same age,
and we were like sisters.

I took her head between my hands, whispered my love in
her ear, and rubbed her burning cheek against mine to crush
her tears. I breathed soft words against her temple, and the
trickle of air that carried them stirred her lightest locks, those
on the edge of her hair that were like a child's down. Tenderly
caressing her with my words, I whispered against her skin that
there was nothing to fear, and that, thanks to the hagioscope—
the hole they had made in the wall of the chapel, allowing me
to see the altar and the Eucharistic dove suspended just above
it from my cell—I would at least be able to hear her wedding
ceremony. I calmed her little by little, as one soothes a child.
Hush now, our paths would cross again after death! Unlike

many anchoresses, I was not making a vow of silence, which meant that we would be able to speak to each other until she left. Hush now, after four days of fasting I would be allowed to open the shutter of my window—a much larger opening, which looked out onto the courtyard, and through which I would be fed, even though it was barred.

"Jehanne, my sweet, you will come to visit me behind my bars. Your Pierre has made a fine window for me, surmounted by a seven-stone arch. The archbishop will no doubt be shocked to see such a breach in the wall of my tomb. But your lover refused to build me a robe that would fit me too snugly, as he put it, the kind of suffocating little cell they make in towns for repentant sinners to waste away their days in darkness and solitude. He was sorry to have to leave the floor bare for my tomb to be dug there. In spite of my orders, he tried to pave my cell to protect me from the dampness of the earth and preserve me from insects. I forced him to take those paving stones up again."

In my packed little chapel, the walls of which were already covered in dazzling frescoes, my father and Lothaire stood side by side in the front row. Neither of them gave me so much as a glance. Their eyes remained cruelly lowered.

I stopped as I came level with them, and whispered, "I shall pray for the two of you. You are leaving me in the hands of my beloved, my heavenly Creator. I will pray that you are rewarded and that your sins be forgiven."

Then, prostrate, I attended my own funeral. Surrounded by members of the chapter of Saint-Jean and my brother Benoît, the archbishop celebrated the mass for the dead in the newly risen chapel of Sainte-Agnès. Facing the altar, his arms spread, his tall, lanky figure seeming, from the back, to be elongated by his miter, he spoke to God, and the modulations of his voice overflowed the chapel, turning it into a monumental nave. His solemn voice built a cathedral. Eyes lowered, I received from his hands the body and blood of Christ, and a great joy overcame me. I felt His warmth, His breath upon me, I surrendered to His invisible arms. My breast rose in elation and my tears flooded my smile. I was submerged by divine grace. The silent archbishop became aware of this wave filling me, and God let him share my ecstasy for a moment. He gave me a radiant smile of gratitude. Then he administered extreme unction, blessed my lily-white linen robe, and dressed me in it.

I thought I heard Jehanne weeping at the back of the chapel, where the villeins and serfs were crowded. As there was not enough room, most of them were massed outside, trying to pick up a few crumbs of the ceremony.

Facing my family and its allies, I uttered my vow of perpetual confinement and accepted that only death could put an end to it.

The archbishop led me to my cell, and I lay down in the grave that had been dug there for me. He blessed me once again and threw a little earth over my body to signify my entry, though still living, into the domain of the dead. Then he locked me in and placed his seal on the door. Already, it was no longer a door and would be walled up as soon as he departed.

The bell of Sainte-Agnès rang out for the first time, while the congregation, so large on that day of grace, sang the response: *"Veni sponsa Christi, accipe coronam, quam tibi Dominus praeparavit in aeternum: pro cuius amore sanguinem tuum fudisti."*

The chapel was emptying. Each stroke of the bell vibrated within me before being interrupted by the next, and I waited for the last peal to see how long my body could resonate. It was a question that suddenly meant a lot to me, and I did not want any other thought to distract me from it. And yet I did not hear that last stroke.

T o you who are listening, I want to recount the events as I lived them, without judging the young girl that I then was.

I spent four days in the blackness of my tomb. Some of my sister anchoresses remained in darkness and silence until they died.

Four days without food or water, without company, without anything to excite my senses, four days out of time, four days to drink my tears, and my little mind unfolded like a poppy. Through faith, meditation, fasting, and solitude, it seemed to me that a path had opened in the darkness, a path taken by the cohorts of the dead, and I went after them to the other shore. There I saw souls struggling in the fire of Purgatory. I shared their Gehenna and became convinced that my prayer was consoling them, that it kept the demons at bay and rescued them from their claws. Then I was taken from that terrible sojourn and raised above the clouds. Christ embraced me and led me, still alive, into His extraordinary light. He allowed me to delight in the choir of angels, of which our chanting was merely a pale echo. My soul resounded with the sound of the cymbals of jubilation much longer than my flesh had vibrated on hearing our poor bell of Sainte-Agnès. My faith offered me visions of unequaled beauty, and the time passed so quickly that I did not believe Jehanne when she came and knocked at the shutter to tell me that my fast was over and I could now eat.

Beating with all her might on the wood, she drew me from my ecstasy and told me how important it was to remain moderate and clean my cell to stop the vermin settling in it, and how pointless to put my body to too harsh a test too quickly.

My limbs no longer obeyed me, my flesh had been abandoned too long by my mind. I finally managed to drag myself to the window and summoned the strength to open my shutter. Daylight hit me like a slap.

From that hole of light, Jehanne handed me a small bowl of soup through the bars. I was surprised to see how weak I was: even holding the small container with both hands, I could not stop the liquid from shaking. I slowly drank the burning soup, feeling it descend into my body with each new mouthful.

Having emptied my chamber pot, Jehanne returned with fresh straw. I noticed how red her eyes were, and in a hoarse voice, barely recovered after days of silence, said, "You've been weeping."

"Your father no longer wants to give me to Pierre. He says he won't let me leave and refuses me permission to marry. He says you're going to need me in your tomb, and that the choice you made to wall yourself up has walled me up, too."

"Let him come, I must talk to him."

"He keeps repeating that you're dead! He's forbidden the household to utter your name, he threatens to cut off any tongue that talks of you and swallow it raw. And these are not idle words! Just this morning, he had your beautiful falcon killed and plucked. It'll be served to him for his supper. It's rumored that the poor bird brought him a ribbon it had found in the bracken, on which your name was embroidered. If he blames a falcon for uttering the forbidden word, can you imagine me going to him in his madness with a message from you? He killed a bird he admired, so I don't dare to think what he'd do to someone like me, about whom he cares not a jot. Besides, deep down I know perfectly well that he's right, that God would surely prefer me by your side. The problem, my sweet Esclarmonde, is that there's no more time! Pierre and I anticipated our nuptials somewhat, and no blood has flowed from me for several moons now, even though I was careful and smeared an elder tree with my menses at the end of autumn, as they tell us to do in order not to be pregnant. Well, today, that shrub is blooming and I'm bearing fruit. God is punishing me for being unable to wait. Do you think the fruit of my sin will be as ugly as my sin, and that everyone will laugh at the deformity of our little one to punish me for being bad?"

"How many children would be born deformed if God were to mark all those conceived outside wedlock, or during the impurity of women, or even during the forbidden days? Only men are cruel enough to make mothers responsible for their children's defects. And besides, God knows what He's doing, He wouldn't have sent Pierre to build this chapel if He had wanted otherwise. In truth, He is urging you to leave this place. When you are gone from here, your younger sister Ivette will take care of me, she will give me my bowl, my water, and some straw for my little cell. She may be simpleminded, but I know she is diligent and kind. Is Lothaire still our guest?"

"Yes. He wanders alone like a lost soul, and seems to have forgotten the way to his own land. He's changed a lot since you've been shut away. He's stopped bothering the girls and talks only to himself."

"Well, as my father has no desire to visit his daughter's tomb, go fetch Lothaire. Tell him that Esclarmonde wishes to see him."

In that time, thousands stirred themselves to visit the relics of Saint Foy or of Mary Magdalene, whose body had been found at Vézelay. This latter saint, who had known Christ, was becoming the symbol of redemption. Between Heaven and Hell, a third place had taken shape, at the entrance to which she stood guard. Thanks to the communion of saints, the baptized—limbs of a single body—could benefit from the sacrifices, prayers, and sufferings of a few sublime, charitable souls. Saints and mystics had the ear of God, and they could stay His arm and redeem sinners. No one dared anger them. I knew that Lothaire would obey my voice, which was now so powerful.

He came, meekly following Jehanne, his eyes bowed as if on his way to communion. His face seemed to me to have grown thinner, and his drawn features expressed a sadness I found touching. He had become so humble that he was barely the same person.

"I have prayed a great deal for you, Lothaire, in my new dwelling. I know what my decision has cost you. But if Christ has chosen me, it is partly because, knowing the ways of your heart, He wished to put you to the test. Are you yourself aware how much you have changed? You are transfigured, resplendent—quite unlike that vain, cruel young man who disgusted me. You needed that wound to cleanse your soul."

"I've turned my heart toward the Lord and taken my eyes from your face. But a single glance would revive my anger and my pain. The Devil is never far, whispering his little song in my ear."

"I want you to go to my father and demand that he give you my foster sister Jehanne as a maidservant, in compensation for the wife you did not get. He won't be able to refuse you such a favor. He'll uproot Jehanne from his fiefdom. But you won't keep her, you'll free her so that she can marry Pierre, the stonecutter, and they can both leave for Paris, where a cathedral is being built."

"I am very honored that you are putting me thus to the test and entrusting this girl to me, knowing the use I have made of women until today."

"I repeat, you have changed, Lothaire. One would have to be blind not to notice the light you bear at present on your brow."

"It is my pain that I bear, the fire that has been eating away at me since you escaped me, a flame that still demands the share that has been stolen from it."

"Oh, Lothaire, you may wish you were bad, but you are not, not anymore! And even if you were, what could you do to me? Where I am now, nobody can touch me."

"You are not my wife, therefore you will be my lady! As the songs say, love does not blossom in marriage. It was when you rejected me in church that love struck me like lightning."

"You ought to choose a more substantial lady for yourself, one whose robe would be easier to lift. Now leave me, you have much to do. And above all, do not utter my name when you see my father, unless you want to end up in the salting tub."

Obeying my word as a woman, Lothaire went to see my father, who, with the agreement of the archbishop, gave him Jehanne without balking. Lothaire then freed my foster sister of her bondage.

At my request, the wedding of Jehanne and Pierre was celebrated not far from me, on the square outside my chapel of Sainte-Agnès.

It did not rain that morning and Benoît was able to join their hands in the sunlight.

J ehanne left for Paris on foot with her meager bundle and an already round belly, which, with a laugh, she had let me feel through my little window.

We were separated for good. She, in motion through the world, would make the roads her dwelling. She would cross the country, measuring creation by her strides, living beneath the sky like a foreigner, working as she went, halting wherever Pierre and his father found employment. She would go beyond the great crucifix that marked the end of this land and blocked the horizon, and her walk would have no limits other than her fatigue and that of her companions and their mules. She would swell the wave of walkers, that nomadic population composed of knights errant, fugitives, minstrels, journeymen, and pilgrims. Those who dragged their crosses, those who cut their ties, those who walked to find redemption. And I, I would remain in my cell, contemplating the worlds that Christ gave me to see, absorbed in my own vertical journey, my ascension through prayer, and everyone would know where to find me, as they know where to find a mill or a tomb. She would be a living word flung to the wind and already flown, and I a heavy word carved in stone.

I would so miss her love and friendship!

Contrary to what I had imagined, I was not alone in my retreat. Every day, as soon as I opened my shutter, I received many a visit. Every day my mutilated ear would listen patiently to our people's confidences as they implored me to pray for their salvation or that of their loved ones. And my soul, which heard their sins better than anyone, would turn to Christ and try to obtain forgiveness for them through the strength of my tears. But I devoted most of my time to the adoration of the Eucharist, my eyes on the altar of the chapel and its dove, full of compassion for the sufferings of Christ. Every morning, thanks to the hagioscope, that small orifice looking into the nave, I was able to participate in the mass celebrated by my brother Benoît, and he would then feed me the Body of Christ through the bars of my window and pray beside me while I entered, through the miracle of the honey-flavored host, into communion with Jesus. Once I had recovered from my ecstasy, we would talk about my visions, my journeys into the other life, and the Holy Scriptures, but words were often powerless to render the force of what went through me, finding its way between my body and my soul. At night, I would imagine Benoît in the solitude of his cell, sitting down with his reed pen and writing down my ecstatic adventures in Latin. I liked to think that, thanks to this passionate scribe, my mystical experiences in the gap between worlds, and the words that Christ dictated to me, would serve others, and that my name and pronouncements might still be uttered after my death. It was important in my day not to forget the names of the dead. The abbey of Cluny, on which my brother's little priory depended, had built its power on its books of the dead—at services, the monks took turns in tirelessly repeating the patronymics of those who had paid to appear on the mortuary rolls so that remission of their sins could be prayed for until the end of time.

As time went on, it became harder to tell whether it was my brother who was directing my conscience or I who was directing his.

In truth, the idea having formed in me that it was my task to guide sinners through the darkness, I was gradually becoming a prophetess. I had convinced myself that by seeing them naked before my window I was able to see into their souls, that Christ was opening their hearts to me, and that I could easily read even the best-hidden sins in them. As I never condemned anyone, and everyone left feeling lighter, my mercy soon gave me a reputation that attracted people from the neighboring fiefdoms.

After only a few months, pilgrims on the way to Rome or Santiago de Compostela began to make a detour by way of Hautepierre in order to meet the anchoress, and so great was their faith that even my father's anger could not chase them all away.

How I liked those people who crisscrossed the Christian world, sticks in hand! In spite of that multitude of tongues and dialects that resulted from the fall of Babel, we always found a way to understand each other, especially as my brother was teaching me Latin, which allowed me to converse with the most learned of these pilgrims. I was an excellent pupil, so gifted for languages that this too added to my reputation of being a woman touched by grace. I had never received so much, talked so much, even in the days when I was still alive and had had to keep to my chamber, embroider, sing, and obey my father. All these souls in movement came to see this woman who had ceased all movement, and life passed before me even though I had left it. I learned much about men and their desires and fears. I was even entrusted with messages for others who would pass later on the road to Compostela, and I would make sure that bread, soup, and wine were given to the most destitute. Many were those who, never having had anything, or having abandoned or lost everything on the journey, begged for their sustenance so that they could continue on their way.

I stood there like a marker at the crossroads of worlds.

At first, my body weakened considerably, it took it several moons to become accustomed to this new life and for the nauseas that seized me every morning to cease. I often vomited when my innards were empty, and at such times it seemed to me that my flesh was being purged of its bad humors.

During those early days, in spite of the cramped nature of my cell, in spite of the pains of my flesh, which constantly reminded me of its presence, in spite of the poverty I was imposing on myself, there was only one occasion when I doubted.

Toward the end of August, as I was speaking with a woman whose face had been eaten away by smallpox and who was on her way to the tomb of Saint Peter, I noticed a wild strawberry on the ground, in the shade of a tree.

A delicate red dot in all that green. I plunged into that tiny gap.

Outside my window, the woman was pouring forth her sins, weeping greatly as she did so.

A wild strawberry, infinity within reach of my mouth.

As my visitor revealed all, overwhelming me with the weight of her words, my mind wandered back in time.

As a child, I had been allowed to leave the castle precincts with my mother and a few girls from the household in search of these nuggets. I loved so much to comb through the bracken, to stir the old leaves. On all fours in the moss like a little beast, I would sniff the earth of the undergrowth and soak up its heady scent. But the most persistent sensation—just to evoke it intoxicates me still today—is my mother's caress, her gentle gesture as her white fingers slipped between my lips the little scarlet pearl she had just plucked—delicately, so as not to crush it.

Death has passed, our bodies have dissolved, but her watchful gaze and her smile still mingle with the taste of the wild strawberry. That tiny fruit concentrates in its heart the flavor of the forest and my mother's love. As the pulp burst between my teeth, it seemed to me that I was communing with the big trees, and that what my mother had given me, as well as a confirmation of her love, was a kind of host.

The woman's words had dried up, her poor prattle had ceased. I must have blessed her without even thinking, since she had already risen and gone on her way. I was ashamed of my distraction, but my daydream would not let go of me.

How I had missed that love!

I realized it on that late afternoon in summer as I looked from my cell at that inaccessible fruit, that minuscule detail vibrant with slightly acidic sweetness, and I hoped that my mother's hands would once more find their way to me and offer me that joyous gift.

Suddenly, Ivette's bare feet, as she brought me my soup and my portion of bread on her way home, tore me from my profane contemplation, almost crushing that delightful memory, stamping on my childhood, my carbuncle. I thanked the girl, all the while wishing that she would leave again as soon as possible and leave me to that precious evocation, in communion not with God but with my mother's perfumed ghost in the form of a strawberry. I imagined that the fruit would lead me to her, to the stories she had told me as a child, that the door would open on her loving gaze.

As Ivette walked away, she noticed that blood red droplet between the leaves. She bent down, plucked it from its little stem, and gobbled it whole. To share this happiness, she turned toward me, and her thin lips opened like curtains on her unsightly teeth, which jostled in her mouth and grew in all directions—every time she let her joy appear in this way, her smile struck down her beauty as surely as any grimace. Without malice, she had just swallowed my mother and the forest before my very eyes, making short work of both of them.

All that remained to me of those lovely days was the shade of a big tree. My mother's hand was in the ground, the forest would be forever invisible, and the door had closed again. I wept.

L othaire often visited the Whispers to pay court to the anchoress. He was now writing poems, which he recited for me in a low voice. He was even learning to sing, the better to charm my ear. I felt a great deal of pity for that wicked young man who said he could no longer sleep because of me and begged for my smiles, as if they were nourishment for him.

"I've been told you no longer deflower young girls in the woods," I said to him one day.

"I've grown up. You buried my desire in a stone coffin when you married the greatest of lords, and now my only wish is to please you. My heart is caged up on this side of the world. It hurts me greatly that I cannot join you. If only your hand would lower itself to stroke my brow, it would stamp it with a wild rapture."

"My hands are dead to caresses, but tonight they will join and pray for you. You have a lovely voice."

"That's because I've engaged an excellent minstrel to teach me. Did you know that I've exchanged the finest of my swords for a vielle? Not that it's easy to play when all one has learned before is the art of war."

"What does your father think of that?"

"That I'm ridiculous and effeminate! He says I'm even worse than my brother Amey, who was so hurt when his betrothed was married to another. He's astonished at my feelings for you, and counts them a weakness. That's why he wants to send me off on the Crusade to fight beside the emperor, who'll soon be leaving with the largest army of all time to wrest Christ's tomb from the hands of Saladin."

"Perhaps you should obey him."

"I couldn't be deprived of you for such a long time. It is you I will lay siege to until I die, not Jerusalem. I know perfectly well that these bars separating us will never fall, that no siege ladders will ever breach them, but this is the only place where I'm happy, because I can hear you."

"You must go now. Many others wish to meet me. I've offered myself to Christ in order to help sinners and pray unceasingly."

"Then I leave you to your task. May I return soon?"

"Whenever you see fit!"

Gentleness had gradually crept into Lothaire's pale blue eyes, and from one conversation to the next, one song to the next, I saw him turn into a man I could have loved.

T he fine days went by so quickly, the summer dissolved in the reading of holy books and in contemplation and prayers and encounters. My self-crucifixion through reclusion was my way of thanking God. Every pain brought me closer to Him, every mortification elevated me. My faith fed on my abnegation and my suffering. I lived with my knees on the ground.

I spotted no more wild strawberries, yet, in spite of the thickness of the walls, I could see, in the rectangular frame of my window, a small part of the castle's courtyard, with the fine maple in the middle, and even, moving my face as close as possible to the bars, a piece of the sky just above. Sometimes, in autumn, the low sun passed between the red leaves of the big tree and found its way to me as I knelt at the crossroads of the living and the dead.

Pierre had built a chimney for me in the wall, a supreme luxury that allowed me not to suffer too much from the cold. I had drained all the bile from me, and the vomiting fits had finally ceased, but I still suffered terribly from hunger, and as soon as I attempted to impose a more severe fast on myself I would feel dizzy and be unable to pray. All the same, I managed to refuse gifts from my visitors. I had decided to stem the flow of these visitors in any case, and now only received them between nones and vespers, to prevent my worship from being constantly interrupted by these waves of penitents.

Even though there was nothing in my cell but an iron chamber pot, a porcelain bowl, a small container for drawing water, an oil lamp, a solid wooden chair, and the straw-filled pit where I slept, it was relatively snug compared with those of some anchoresses in towns, who did not even have enough space to lie flat on the floor and had, or so I was told, either to keep standing or to sit with their feet in the mire, so that their bodies crawled with vermin. Their heads did not even reach the level of the tiny windows placed so high that the only glimpse afforded them of the outside world was, at best, an absurdly small square of sky. Visitors were unable to communicate with them, and had to be content with hearing their prayers. The townspeople would throw them bread as they passed, in gratitude for their sacrifice. Whenever I thought of these sisters of mine, I felt ashamed that my cell was so spacious, so clean, so warm, my window so wide, and that my simpleminded Ivette took such good care of me.

Although I ate less than a bird, my body seemed swollen and heavy to me, and I felt as though I were dragging it along with me. I could understand neither how the air could enter my entrails in such a way as to make my belly swell, nor how the other anchoresses were able to preserve their vigilance in conditions so much more difficult than mine.

In the fifth month of my reclusion, I felt movements in my belly. They were not painful, but totally new and uncontrollable. Something was struggling within me. And as the weeks passed, these disturbances became more and more noticeable, and more and more frequent. My body, to which I had paid very little attention, was changing. It took me a long time to accept the fact, and even longer to understand the reason. In spite of the frugality of my meals, my belly, which was as hard as stone, kept growing ever rounder, and my skin was soon stretched to breaking point. The agitation that sometimes shook it was eventually perceptible from the outside. When I placed my hands on my belly, I could feel the distortions imposed upon it by whatever was stirring there.

What demon was stirring my entrails in this way, devouring me from within? There was something inside me, something throbbing, something that moved beneath my skin like a hand beneath a sheet.

I had not bled since I had been walled up, and had been innocent enough to believe that this cessation of the menses was linked to my reclusion, that God had delivered me from what the clerics called the periodic impurity of woman. That blood I no longer lost was swelling my veins, which now undulated, thick and blue, across my emaciated body.

The reality struck me so abruptly that I thought I would faint. How could I have been blind for so long?

I could no longer fool myself: Christ had decided not to relieve me of the burden of pregnancy.

And I had thought I was safe from the devil in my tomb!

What was I going to do, alone within these walls with a child's head wedged between my legs? The baby would have to come out, and I was so ignorant.

Nobody must know!

It was easy to hide my condition from all those who knelt before my window and demanded my help, for they saw only my face and shoulders. But what would happen later? What would I do with a bouncing baby if, by some miracle, we both survived? The anxiety soon became so strong that it would have driven me mad if I had not overcome it. Faced with this unthinkable situation, I had only one resource left to me: to give myself up to God. He would take care of everything, I convinced myself. Confidently, I accepted this new trial.

My occupier no longer terrified me. Gradually, it became familiar to me. Whenever the child moved at night, I would imagine that it was afraid of the dark. I would pray out loud, and it would calm down, doubtless accompanying me in my prayer. By day, at the hour when I received visitors, I would feel it playing in my belly, and that made me smile.

From time to time, I had news of Jehanne. She would visit anchoresses in the towns she passed through and ask them to get a few words to me. In my century, these women, confined behind walls as they were, had great power. Thanks to their network, her words reached me, carried by the pilgrims, transformed by the dialects and accents and oversights of the messengers. I could see my foster sister's large black eyes behind these strangers' faces, and hear her laughter in their voices. Few anchoresses' cells were as isolated as mine—most were in towns or convents—and yet the noise of the world came to my window, and that noise was filled with our words, Jehanne's and mine. What a joy it was to hear her words in other people's mouths and to entrust my answers to good people who would make sure they reached Vézelay, for it was there that she had stopped and brought her little Paul into the world! I even managed to get several letters to her in this way, knowing that she would be sure to find someone to read them to her.

My son was born a few days before Easter, as the maple spread its tender leaves and the box trees were already being marked out to be cut and blessed during mass on Palm Sunday. My fruit had taken its time. It arrived well before the first light of dawn, and in order to stop myself from crying out I put a cloth in my mouth and a piece of wood between my teeth like a bit.

On Ash Wednesday, I had questioned my old nurse, Jehanne's mother, about how children are born. I had sent for her after the mass and she had come to my window. On her brow, beneath the silvery mass of her hair, was the cross of ashes that my brother had drawn on it with his thumb. "Remember that thou art dust and to dust thou shalt return." Her piercing eyes, their indefinable color made lighter by age, had not left mine as she explained in detail what I should do: the pains, the position to take, the moments to push, the head to be turned to let the shoulders through, the cord to be cut, the wait for the afterbirth. It occurred to me that, speaking to me in that way, she must have guessed my condition. I had no polished metal mirror, nor anybody I could ask if I bore the mask of pregnant girls—that brown that comes to the cheeks of some as early as the first months and is recognized by the older women. And yet, even if I had been thus marked in the face, who could have imagined that Esclarmonde, the virgin, concealed a fruit? Whatever she understood, the good woman had never spoken of it to anybody. But she had discreetly made sure that after compline I always had either a lighted tallow candle or nut oil for my lamp, and that I lacked for neither water nor wood. I had even had the impression, starting on the very day after our conversation, that the soup Ivette brought me had grown noticcably thicker, which had surprised me somewhat, given that it was the beginning of Lent.

Thanks to the fire, I was able, as soon as I felt the pains coming, to put water on to boil in my iron pot and pour it into my bowl, taking care not to burn myself. I did my best with what little I had, and Christ saw to the rest. The spasms gradually increased during the night. I struggled for hours in my solitude to contain a pain for which I had prepared myself, but whose intensity was greater almost than I could bear. Between one cramp and the next, I made sure that my fire did not go out, with the result that my cell became as hot as an oven. I swallowed my cries until they choked me and I lost consciousness. The singing of angels awoke me, and I found the strength to undress in order not to soil my tunic, to crouch in the straw and catch the head of the child as it made its way out. It tore me slightly as it emerged from my body and a last silent scream lacerated my throat.

It was a boy.

Blinded by the sweat that ran into my eyes, I cut the cord with that same little knife I had used to truncate my wedding, and when the warm sticky child gave his first cry I wrapped him in a clean piece of linen that a pilgrim had given me and that I had accepted in preparation for this moment. In my time, it was only that first cry that was considered the beginning of life. If babies had no voice, it was a terrifying prospect. It meant that they lacked breath, they were not part of the air, it was as if they had been stopped at the entrance to the world, and they were not deemed to be alive as long as they had not declared themselves. My son was very much alive, he was crying himself hoarse in my tomb.

I realized that this little red thing was howling for my teat, so I stuffed it into his mouth to silence him, in a panic lest his screams awaken the household.

I suffered a little more until the afterbirth emerged, then recovered my breath, trembling and exhausted in the silence of the night.

Looking down at the profile of the newborn clutching my breast, the softness of that curve, the quivering of his lips, I suddenly felt my heart leap with joy and love for this new creature whose mother I was and who depended entirely on me. As he suckled and his tiny fingers moved over my skin, I finally agreed to ask myself the essential questions.

Even before giving this child a name, I had to think. I had to find a way either to justify his presence or to get him away from there. He would pass easily enough through the vertical bars of the window, and I could put him down on the outer sill and make everyone believe that he was a child abandoned outside my cell. No local woman would be allowed to enter my tomb and verify my virginity again. For a moment, I considered entrusting the baby to my brother Benoît, so that he could leave it in some monastery. But he was much too small still, and the monks would not agree to take charge of him. The best solution was to give him to Ivette, who would find a nurse for him and demand that my father pay for the maintenance of this creature left outside my window. The most important thing was that he should be baptized as soon as possible, so afraid was I of condemning his soul to damnation—one of those terrible, visceral fears your contemporaries can no longer understand.

My father had not yet put in an appearance outside my cell. In the autumn, he had taken a second wife, a young childless widow not much older than myself, whom I had often glimpsed since her arrival at the castle. Her name was Douce, and she smiled at me whenever she passed beneath the maple, but, doubtless in obedience to her husband, she kept her distance, and merely slowed down when she crossed my field of vision to get to her patch of medicinal plants—Bérengère, her massive maidservant who always wore green skirts, knew about herbs, it was said, and had had all kinds of them planted near my ornamental garden. It was rumored that Douce was afraid of sleep, and that Bérengère would lie down at night across the door of the bridal chamber to reassure her. It was also whispered that my father tripped over the big girl every time desire overcame him and he left his bed to join some wench or other. How he must have cursed that strange sentry!

Surely it was time the Lord of the Whispers came to pray over his daughter's tomb?

But would he make peace with God? Would he agree to take care of an orphan abandoned before my burial place? And would he see the features of his own lineage in the child's face?

I named the baby Elzéar, God's help.

With some difficulty, I managed partly to bury, partly to burn in the hearth, the traces of his birth. The fire gave off a terrible smell of burned flesh, which fortunately faded before sunrise.

The bells rang for lauds and, as I did every morning, I gave thanks to God for this new dawn that was breaking.

I continued with my prayers all day without opening my shutter, letting the child suckle or walking him back and forth in my tomb as soon as he threatened to cry, in order to avoid anyone guessing what was happening in my cell. I could not make up my mind about the course to take.

When evening fell, overcome with exhaustion, I fell asleep in spite of myself. Elzéar did not break my sleep, and I did not wake in the night to pray, nor did I even hear the matins bell.

When I finally awoke, I was so hungry and thirsty that my

thoughts became confused. I could not keep my shutter closed much longer. The child had drained me of my milk, and had stopped crying in spite of his soiled swaddling clothes and my dried-up nipples. I thought that he was dying and, suddenly driven wild by the fear that he might expire, I tried to call to Benoît, who was celebrating mass in the chapel. My little one had to be baptized immediately! But almost nothing emerged from my throat. The labor of childbirth had stolen my voice, and I could no longer cry out. Only Elzéar heard my rasping moan, his eyelids opened, and he looked at me with that intensity, that wisdom, that wonderful calm that babies' eyes have. He curbed my anxiety, and I realized that, even if I confessed that the child was mine, nobody, apart from his father, would be able to explain the mystery of his birth. So I would not have to lie, but only to keep silent about what I had already kept silent about until then!

They would leave me my child for as long as his head could pass between the bars. Doubtless a year, perhaps longer!

How I must have suffered from being deprived of caresses, tenderness, and human warmth, to even dream of keeping a child confined in such a sad place!

The idea of postponing my separation from my newborn was so attractive to me that at first this possibility prevailed in my heart. But how many months, how many years would we have before he was either walled up with me or separated from me forever? Before he became too big either to escape from this belly of stone or to return to it? The flesh splits and tears, and iron bars are even worse than hips that are too narrow.

And would they allow an anchoress to keep a newborn child in her tomb?

I had never before heard of a such a woman giving birth to a child more than nine moons after she had died to the world. It would seem like a miracle! The father would not come forward. His fury had doubtless passed, the devil that had inspired his crime in the mist had left him. If he had wanted to speak up, he would have done so earlier. He would let people believe whatever they wished. He may even have been too drunk on the morning of his sin to remember it.

The child had miraculously emerged from my belly during the night and that was all!

And yet what a falsehood it would be! In thus deceiving those around me, would I not be distancing myself from the goal I had set?

I finally decided to sacrifice my joy, to fetch my father, to confess to him that this child was mine and entrust him to his care.

Never before had I sent for him.

That Friday morning, then, I took the risk of opening my shutter and asking Ivette for a drink. She had been watching over me beneath the foliage of the great maple, distaff in hand, worried at seeing my window closed since the day before yesterday, but far too respectful to dare knock at it. Elzéar was again asleep in the straw, his little fists clenched. I knew now that he was indeed alive. His eyes had swept away my fear. After Ivette had filled my water container and brought a more copious meal than usual, a meal I had not had the strength to refuse, I ordered her to go to my father and tell him that Esclarmonde was demanding to see him as soon as possible. My God, how the poor girl trembled at the thought of reminding the lord that the woman whose name nobody in his household dared utter in his presence was still alive! Ivette did not dare shirk my request, or even express any reservation, but I saw the terror in her usually calm grey eyes. I felt I had to encourage her in order for her to carry out her errand, and I made her promise that she would serve me unflinchingly. My father was just then passing beneath the maple, and I entreated Ivette to speak to him there and then. She left me, walking unsteadily, sure that she would be beaten by the master. She had already witnessed some of his rages, and knew what that simple sentence with which I had entrusted her could bring about, that whispered sentence now filling her mouth like burning liquid. Head down, she approached the lord and laid my message at his feet. He did not beat her, no, he did not even raise his voice, he said nothing in reply, merely cast a glance in my direction—the first in so long that I had forgotten the icy brightness of his eyes—before continuing on his way with a slightly different step, as if the words uttered by Ivette still clung a little to his heels.

I heard his answer without his having needed to utter a word. He would come.

Several hours passed before he returned from the hunt and I savored that interval, I chewed on every second, clinging to Elzéar, enjoying the warmth of his skin against mine—to touch, to caress, to embrace, how sweet that carnal contact was to me after all those months of separation from bodies!—watching out for the angelic smiles on his peaceful little face, offering myself that last pleasure of feeling him sleeping trustingly in my arms, mouth half open. I was drunk on trifles: the smell of his hair, the smallness of his feet, his fingers with their perfectly-formed nails, the folds of flesh at his wrists, the little blister he had in the middle of his lip from all that sucking. I blew into his neck, kissed every inch of his body, and refused to think. It was the only way to stop my resolve from falling apart.

Father suddenly beat with his fist against my shutter, startling me.

It was time to offer Elzéar a future, a future in which I would have no place.

Father stood framed in the window, against the light, and his shadow entered my cell, his shadow crawled over my skin, spread over my body, went beyond it, and stretched across the floor before breaking in the corner and rising long and thin behind me all the way up the back wall. His shadow covered me entirely, it erased me. Against the light, his dark, massive silhouette concealed the outside world. I could not see his face, his eyes. My father was not the Devil, I thought, even though he might like to pretend he was, and I had grown: no man would ever again be able to crush me beneath him as he moaned. A shadow, even that of a once loving, now humiliated father, would never have the strength others attributed to it. Those huge hands projected onto my skin would take nothing from it but the light.

"So you never meditate over the tomb of Esclarmonde!"

"I have nothing to say, nothing to ask, either of the ghost of my daughter or even of God."

"Well, your daughter certainly has something to say to you! I gave birth to this child last night, and I'd like you to take care of him as if he were your own. I've named him Elzéar. It's up to you to find a way to justify his presence. His fate and mine are in your hands."

I then handed him my little bundle of cloth and flesh, gently easing it between the bars. I gave up my poorly wrapped child to that fearsome man, who, caught off guard, did not at first know what to do with him. The sleeping infant managed a smile.

Once he had recovered from his surprise, Father slipped the baby beneath the red velvet of his cloak, then, without another word, turned on his heels and set off with a determined step in the direction of the castle.

I watched, powerless, as my child was taken away, aware that I would probably never see him again. I understood the pain to which God had condemned women since the Fall. Childbirth was not only physical torture, it was a mixture of intense joy and fear as heavy as a stone. Mothers knew that death was already at work as soon as their child took its first breath, as if clinging to its delicate flesh. Remember that thou art dust!

I still had his smell on my hands, the softness of his skin on my fingertips, the imprint of his head on my shoulder. The thin skin of my breasts, where all my humors were suddenly gushing, would tear like cloth, and my body would soon burst from the excess of love and milk contained within it.

That hollow in my arms was like an emptiness in my soul!

And, for the first time, God was of no help to me. Had He abandoned me as I had just abandoned my son? I tried to pray to fill the vast solitude. But nothing could overcome a sorrow too great to hold entire in my body, to hold entire in that small room or in the minuscule landscape framed by my window. It seemed to me that only the forest could have contained such a desert.

The now absent Elzéar had filled me so full that God no longer had a place.

Against all expectation, my father's shadow reappeared again in my cell, a restless shadow, shaken by cries. The Lord of the Whispers stood there stiffly, facing me, and through the bars he handed me Elzéar, who was screaming in pain.

"I give you back your child, you and that God who has made you both His daughter and His bride. Don't count on me to give Him more than I have just given Him!"

As my father walked away, I gathered my child, whom I had thought lost, in my arms and tried to calm my treasure by putting him to my breast, but my milk could not quench his cries, which were already drawing people from the castle. Terrified by my infant's shrill screams and taking no heed of the silent crowd that was starting to form outside my cell, I placed him on the inner sill of my window in order to be more at ease to free his sweet little body from the cloth in which he had been so clumsily wrapped. It was then that I saw that his tiny hands were bleeding, and I suddenly realized what my father had done to him.

Those jostling outside the window to witness the scene discovered his palms at the same time as I did.

A murmur spread through the gathering.

A murmur of astonishment and terror.

His palms had been pierced through.

I was very young then, young and silly and completely powerless in the face of my son's inarticulate pain. Refusing my
breast, Elzéar was screaming so much that tears came to
my eyes. And the people of the castle, once over their amaze-
ment, called to others and ran off in all directions to announce
the news, this second miracle after the lamb. Nobody seemed
to have seen my father give me back this little one, whom he
had tortured, nobody had noticed that he was running away
like someone who knows perfectly well that he has committed
a sin. Elzéar's glow, his pierced hands, his hands like stars in a
beam of light, had removed any last doubt. His cherubic fair
hair and exceptional complexion contrasted so violently with
the poverty and darkness of my cell that this image alone
would no doubt have sufficed to leave its mark on everyone.

I remained silent, thinking only of cradling, thinking only
of praying. My old nurse, Jehanne's mother, approached my
window and everyone stepped aside to make way for her. As
the oldest member of the community, she asserted herself—
with her quiet strength, her common sense and her herbs—as
the only person able to tend to those pierced little hands.
Unconcerned with any question of miracles, she asked me for
Elzéar in a gentle but firm voice, laid him on the outside sill,
keeping the mass of gawping onlookers at a distance with a
gesture, placed plasters on the child's palms, and wrapped
him comfortably in a fresh cloth before giving him back to me.
My little one, that bringer of joy and fear that God had given

me, calmed down, and even fell asleep against my breast, a trickle of foam, white with milk, at the corner of his half-open mouth.

And as he slept, the rumor swelled, rumbled, spread through the fiefdom of the Whispers, the rumor went beyond the great crucifix, crossed the horizon, bounced from family to family, from town to town, took to the main road, cut across fields, one mouth reached twenty ears, which immediately became as many tongues, and everyone hastened to repeat, to tell, to invent this miracle in his own way, with his own words, adding details: holes in the feet, a crown of thorns, golden haloes around my head and Elzéar's, and a new star in the sky, a bluish star so brilliant that some asserted they had seen it at high noon and been blinded by it long enough to recite two hundred Ave Marias. Esclarmonde, the walled-up virgin, had given birth to a little angel that Friday, they declared in ecstasy, and the miraculous child bore the stigmata of Christ, spoke Latin, recited the Gospels, and had already cured two lepers and three paralytics.

"Rejoice!" cried hydra-headed Rumor at the top of her voice. "God has given the world a wonderful gift!"

The more the hours passed, the more fabulous the story became, the longer the list of miracles performed by the child, the more elaborate, structured, and detailed the legend. Everyone contributed toward it, adding his own inspiration, competing with everyone else in invention, and the whole thing flourished all the more easily as Easter was approaching.

How could I extricate myself from all that?

The very next day, I would have to explain myself to the clerics, that much was certain, and I had no idea what I should say.

Ivette had washed my child and rubbed his body with salt and flower oil, and his mouth and nostrils had kept the smell and taste of the maple and oak honey she had put on them.

I spent my night in prayer, kneeling on the ground, rising only to feed Elzéar, my limbs aching, numb from having stooped too long, imploring God, who was suddenly deaf and distant, to inspire me, caressing my child's smooth, full cheeks, surprised at so much pain, and knowing now what a torment it would be to be separated from him. I hoped that he would live, and I looked for a way to shield him from my father's hatred and the Devil's clutches.

I refused to lie. Nevertheless, Elzéar's destiny would be shaped by my words, and as soon as I revealed the truth he would be torn from me. Yes, they would force me out of my cell to undergo torture, I would have to give up the name of his father and explain where his stigmata came from, and we would all end up on the same stake.

What, then, had I been looking for by entering within these walls? A mystic ecstasy, the proximity of God, the splendor of sacrifice, or the freedom I had been refused by being offered in marriage?

Was I not about to lose everything if I let this living lie bind my soul?

My certainties were collapsing, my faith was falling apart in this torment of thoughts, and all the while my child was smiling angelically, perfectly satisfied.

Was this child merely the fruit of frustration and hate? Could it be that, in giving myself sincerely to God, I had provoked such a disaster? This wave of madness would carry us all away like wisps of straw in the blast of a fire!

How the Devil must be laughing about all this, the corruption of my faith, the reversal in my soul! Doubtless he was trying once again to separate me from God. My cell was becoming the scene of a battle he was fighting with the Almighty. A battle in which this child seemed to be the prize. I could not let the enemy take Elzéar away, I could not give him both my son and my father with the same words. No, I would thwart the demon's plans. All I would have to do was be silent and demonstrate my lack of understanding.

Everything would depend on what Father said. If he confessed his sin, he would condemn all three of us to opprobrium, but if he said nothing, what would become of his soul? Would my prayers suffice to save him? To save us?

Christ was love, Christ could see into my heart, Christ would protect us! Doubt must not be allowed to interfere!

I prayed.

A cry rent the night, the cry of pain and terror of a damned soul, and that cry immediately found its companion. A woman's shrill scream joined it, piercing the darkness.

T he next day, my stepmother, Douce, made her way through the people who were kneeling a dozen steps from my cell, waiting respectfully for my window to open, and scratched at the shutter like a little animal.

"Your father is in a very bad way," she murmured through the cracks. "He tried to crucify himself on the head of our bed last night. He nailed his left hand, then, realizing he was unable to continue by himself, held out the hammer to me and ordered me to plunge the second nail into his other palm. I refused. To the head of the bed! He is dreaming awake and speaks without seeing me, writhing about in the grip of terrible visions. He is naked and terrifying. I tremble at the thought of approaching him, having disobeyed him. He threatens to bite me as soon as I try to free him. I've forbidden everyone in the household to enter our bedchamber. You alone could aid him, your name recurs endlessly in his delirium. I beg you, help me to restore his reason!"

I laid Elzéar in my straw-filled pit and opened my shutter to answer those lips that were whispering into the wood as if into an ear. My father had to recover from his sin, but above all we had to find a way to silence him.

My stepmother was already fully dressed, her hair completely concealed in an immaculate wimple, her fingers covered in rings, and her scent wafted into my cell, borne on the light breeze that stirred her veils. Moving as close to me as she could, perfect in spite of the early hour, even though her voice throbbed with anguish, my young stepmother was speaking to me for the first time. Beneath her pale, smooth brow, as large as a sky, her tears could not adulterate the darkness of her pupils.

"Douce, what a joy to meet you at last! Tell my father that he has misinterpreted the will of God. To follow the cross does not mean crucifying yourself in your chamber, it means sewing a cross on your chest. He won't redeem his sins unless he prepares for departure. Let him ask permission of his liege lord, the archbishop, to raise the funds he will need to leave for the Crusade. With that blessing, he will quit the fiefdom and lead his men to Regensburg! He will have to get there before the end of next winter. Tell him that he will find Emperor Frederick there and will follow him to the Holy Land. Tell him that he will leave us in seven months, that his hands will help to liberate Jerusalem, and that if he stays nailed to a bed, he will be as useless to God as to men!"

Douce grimaced, and her tears dried. This woman with her lively eyes had more temperament than I had imagined. It would not be so easy to get her to submit.

"I have only just remarried, and you want to make me a widow again."

"And I would be doubly an orphan!"

"Then why send him away to be killed?"

"There is no place for him in this world, all he has left is to fight to reconquer that which has been reserved for him in the next."

"The Crusades are a kind of bloodletting that balances a country's humors. Let them take the young knights, the younger sons without lands and without wives, whose ardor can no longer be assuaged with tournaments, let them take all those who spread disorder in the earldom and have no respect for the Peace of God! Let them drain it of the young impetuous blood that finds no place in it, the pus of those fools for Christ unable to discharge their own violence, the mucus of the idle, not aging lords who maintain order in their fiefdoms and properties and guarantee stability!"

"We need rational fighters to command those turbulent youths in search of adventure, glory, and lands who will soon be setting off on the roads. My father will leave his anger and madness here, my father will leave his sins and his loved ones here in order to regulate that flood. He will restrain the wildest of the Crusaders, prevent much slaughter, and lead the Christians to victory."

"He will die far from his family."

"Yes, he will die, but at least he will die in the Holy Land, at the gates of Jerusalem."

My stepmother's body stiffened, and even her veils stopped quivering. Only some blue veins throbbed at her temples, swollen by a rising anger. Between her eyebrows, two ugly lines scored her vast forehead.

"I shan't say anything. I don't want him to leave me so soon, I don't want to keep changing households. I feel good here, at the Whispers, and I'm carrying his child. Don't count on me to deprive it of a father! Do you take me for a fool who can be led by the nose? Why should he be involved in that carnage?"

"If he stays, he will die much more quickly. He will die half-crucified, he will die naked, held to his bed by a nail, devoured by anguish. He will die still full of his sins, which are many and very wicked. And we shan't meet him again in the afterlife. You will never see him again. If he stays, he will expire in a cry even more terrifying than the one he let out last night, and that cry will pursue you beyond his death. He will cry for all eternity and nobody will be able to put his soul back together."

"Who do you think you are, trying to move people on the great chessboard of the world as you wish? You don't like your father, so you send him away. He spends one night trapped in a bad dream, and you take advantage of the situation to condemn him."

"And what will become of his line? How will your child be able to honor the memory of that madman, that unworthy father struck down in his bed by invisible demons? Every lord feeds on the fame of his ancestors. For centuries, your ears will echo with the cry of this man whose name you will have tarnished by refusing to be the messenger of God!"

Douce was glowing now like a cold star, her pallor seemed ghostly, her eyes shot their dark rays at me. Controlling her features, she whispered her rage, concentrated it in her words.

"So now you feel so established in your role as a prophetess that you dare to judge other people's souls! Do you think you can scare me, waving my husband's supposed sins in my face and threatening me? You're an ambitious woman, Esclarmonde, you're too fond of leading, of forcing others on particular paths. I shall cure him with the help of herbs! Nobody will ever convince me that you are a saint, nobody will ever convince me that your child was not engendered by a man or that you entered that cell a virgin. All these fools kneeling here are naïve and pathetic, and I find the way you use them shameful. How dare you say that you live in God? You who do nothing but lie to ensure your power!"

"Douce, Douce, your words hurt me. Try whatever you wish. I hope your potions can cure my father, because I love him despite his violence and his sins. But I don't think they'll be much use."

My stepmother's thin lips curved like a saber in the silence. Then she leaned toward me and whispered threateningly, "Take care, girl! You've ventured on a dangerous path. Between the summit and the abyss, there is but one step, and those who climb too high too fast risk a fall. A fall or the gallows!"

That day, the pilgrims, whatever their birth, kept silent. Mouths sealed, they approached my cell one after the other and prostrated themselves, and I saw their eyes search the darkness of my tomb in search of my child. Outside the window, the gifts were piling up, and my chapel was filled with candles

Lothaire came only after all those people were gone.

He did not bow. Ignoring Elzéar, he planted a rosebush brought back from the East against the wall of my chapel and sang me the story of his brother Amey de Montfaucon, consumed with love for the beautiful Berthe, that childhood friend who had been given in marriage to the powerful Amaury de Joux. In his song, women were of no consequence. They all obeyed their fathers and abandoned their tender lovers as soon as they were ordered to do so. Their promises were nothing but vain words. Berthe had married a rough man, a great lord who had never been able to love anything but his horse, a fierce white animal called Gauvin. Without hesitation, the girl had said yes on the square outside the church, knowing it would destroy her dear Amey. The wedding had been celebrated eight years earlier and all the nobility of the earldom of Burgundy had been present. Montfaucon and his family were among the guests. Only Lothaire, that young squire who had returned home to celebrate Amey's dubbing, had remained with the new knight at the castle of Montfaucon. It was he, that boy of twelve, who had discovered his elder brother hanging by the neck from a rope. Amey had just kicked away the stool on which he had been balancing, and his legs were moving in all directions. Without a word, Lothaire had put the stool back under the feet of his brother, who by now was gasping for breath. Once the rope had been loosened, Amey, between two spasms, had revealed the sorrow he had silenced until then, and his violent sadness had struck the child's heart like a leather strap, struck it and made it so hard that no girl would ever again be able to reach it.

When he had developed an appetite, Lothaire had satisfied himself without hesitation or remorse, and, imitating his elders, had picked whichever girls were about—pretty little things whose looks would fade soon enough with a life in the fields. Bouquets of cries, flowers plucked in the woods, some barely open, fragile beneath their petals of rough cloth.

But Esclarmonde was not the kind of girl to abandon and sacrifice her will to the whims or interests of a father, and so, at the altar, Lothaire had been caught up by the feeling he had thought he could escape. Now, in his turn, he was dying of love for a bride who had been stolen from him.

"Dear lady, you have chosen to wed four stone walls, and your sweet body is imprisoned by the coldest of embraces. How can you, with all your beauty, ignore the warmth of my arms and prefer the icy silence of this tomb to my passionate love, my song, my fidelity? Are you so cruel as not to see that I am dying of desire? And that my life stopped the day you rejected me?"

His vielle produced notes so similar to sighs that I smiled at this mad lover.

And yet, that very evening, in the darkness of my cell, I hugged my child's warm body to fight the lingering enchantment of that little song.

I had not grasped how strongly Archbishop Thierry II, who had witnessed what he described as the miracle of the lamb, supported me. The man, a prince in his city, felt as cramped in his office as in his tall, thin frame. In his opinion, the miter stretched his body too much.

As a respite from his huge responsibilities, both political and spiritual, he had chosen two curious pastimes: he loved drawing war machines of all kinds, accumulating unlikely models of siege engines—trebuchets, belfries, battering rams, and mangonels—in one of the halls of his palace, and he also loved the beginnings of the lives of the saints. He had himself begun writing a number of hagiographies, but as he was particularly fond of the beginnings he had never managed to see a martyr's life through to its end. Describing the final sufferings of these good people wearied him, and he would give up, wondering how God had been able to bear being the impassive witness of them. If he had not been so powerful or so formidable, he would certainly have been considered eccentric.

My case excited him, he had accompanied me to the tomb and felt involved in my choice.

No sooner had he had wind of Elzéar's birth than he abandoned his plans for the ingenious trebuchet that would attempt to shake the walls of Acre a few years later and rushed to the Whispers, crozier in hand, dragging his gray little entourage in their cowls, cassocks, and surplices after him at such an infernal pace that they were soon gasping for breath.

Not for a second did he cast any doubt on the idea of a miraculous conception.

Outside my window, he dismissed with a mere gesture of his hand the skepticism of the clerics who had come with him—a slight movement of his fingers sufficiently sharp to silence the astonished hubbub—then, in the silence he had imposed, he said in a low voice that this magnificent child could not be other than a gift of God, that the ways of the Almighty were impenetrable and the story much too good to let human mediocrity tarnish it.

So everyone was content to ask me how Elzéar had come out of my belly but not how he had entered it. I was safe for now, I did not even have to lie, limiting myself to relating how I had given birth in the straw and how I had labored all alone that night, with that cry stuck in my throat, that cry that would wait longer still before escaping me, that cry that would tear my faith apart when at last I would spew it out, laden with all the sorrows about which I had previously kept silent.

"In the straw!" said the archbishop, red-faced with excitement and enthusiasm. "He was born in the straw! Like in a manger!"

His entourage immediately began discussing the gulf that existed between the Virgin and me, Mary having remained a virgin after the birth of Christ, body intact, without a fissure, "vulva and uterus closed." These men, strangers as they were to the secrets of childbirth, were fascinated by the entrails of the mother of God, and for a moment it seemed as if they had forgotten me, so intoxicated were they by this subject. If I had not been so afraid or so naïve, I might have laughed, so incongruous was their chatter. Some, who had entered the monastery very young, had never known any women, let alone rubbed shoulders with them, but that did not prevent them from dictating women's conduct in their ministry, while others had not always been able to keep away from women, in spite of the rope around their cassocks that symbolized their vow of chastity, but all of them were arguing away, sure that they held the truth about that sacred bosom.

"Having kept quite close company with women," one of them asserted, "I still can't understand how Christ could have come out of a woman without taking the usual route. Mary was a virgin before the birth of her son—St. John and St. Matthew say so and nobody has ever doubted it—and according to St. James, her virginity was still intact afterwards, which may be so, and yet it seems to me that door must have opened during the birth."

"You are mistaken!" retorted a thin, pale young monk. "The Virgin is not a woman like any other. Her divine Motherhood is incomparable, Her Holiness unequaled!"

"Her Body does not resemble that of the females you have known," bleated a third man. "Her Womb has neither the coolness nor the dampness that characterize the wombs of other women and are the cause of their despicable inability to assuage their hungers. The knowledge you have of these snakes who rub against men at night in search of warmth makes it impossible for you to know the truth. Only monks who have remained chaste, far from these predators, far from the horror of their flesh and their wanton ways, only such pure men can really appreciate the miracle of the birth of Christ!"

"Here's someone who doesn't even know his own mother," scoffed the man who had spoken first, "and yet he claims to know more than I do about the mother of Jesus!"

"How can you compare the Body of the Virgin to 'those women's bellies stretched by pregnancy and bursting like old wineskins'?"

"Christ wasn't born like us 'surrounded by urine and feces'! Your knowledge of that devil's doorway, a woman's private parts, makes no difference!"

"Tut, tut!" said the archbishop at last. "Come now, my

brothers, enough of this pointless squabbling! This is neither the time nor the place for such reflections."

Thierry II delivered his verdict. He would leave me my son, whose wounds had by now stopped bleeding. Did he imagine that, in thus influencing the course of my existence, he was helping to write the life of a saint? If God refused to intervene to defend his wonders, if he let human stupidity destroy the most beautiful of his creatures, perhaps it was in the hope that a man such as him would eventually recognize them before it came to the fire, the cross, or the stones.

So a tacit agreement was made that no questions be asked about this marvel. Little matter where the child came from— the conditions of this birth were miraculous and this baby, with his extraordinary glow, as if lit from within, this diaphanous little thing with his pierced hands, was seen as a gift from Heaven that the Church would be able to put to good use.

God had sublimated my pain, and my misfortune had turned to gold. For the diocese, this birth was like manna from Heaven. It would attract pilgrims and gifts. The clerics were already rubbing their hands. I was interested in neither manna from Heaven nor the interests of the Church. I was interested only in Elzéar, whose huge eyes stared at me without yet seeing me and who was grimacing so prettily as he moved his tiny fingers around the stigmata given him by my father's madness.

The archbishop, genuinely moved, as much by the child's beauty as by his wounds, asked to baptize him two days later in the chapel of Sainte-Agnès. The man was far from gullible, but he did not doubt my innocence, and I felt that he was trying to protect us from the madness of his contemporaries. For there was a thin line in those days between holiness and heresy. With his hand gloved in white, his fingers laden with huge rings, he blessed us, my son and me, to seal our destiny. Then this strange personage asked to be taken to the quarry, where he wished to take a look at the wheels that had been used to lift the blocks of stone of which the chapel was made and hoist them from the banks of the Loue to the castle. As he walked away from my cell, he was already talking about the *diametros* of the treadwheel cranes and becoming vociferous in his championing of an ingenious system, using several pulleys, which would be far stronger than any man.

T he baptism ceremony stirred the whole region, and people came from far and wide to be present at the event. Never had the Whispers welcomed so many people. Servants, grooms, and guards ran in all directions that day, but they were smiling, delighted in spite of the extra work, proud of belonging to this house and living in the blessed presence of Elzéar and Esclarmonde.

The stables were overflowing, the courtyard so packed that horses, mules, and litters had to be kept beyond the wooden fence. Many of those who had arrived the day before had slept in ditches. Others, more fortunate, had been welcomed inside the castle or had raised their tents beside the fence. Not to mention all those yokels who had come on foot from the four corners of the earldom and cursed under their breaths that they could not get any closer to the chapel. I had left my son with my brother Benoît before the opening of the great gate and closed my shutter to withdraw into myself.

But I could hear the commotion outside: the stamping and snorting of the horses, arguments, reunions, laughter, prayers, insults, and songs.

In those days, mothers were never present at the baptism of their children. They kept to their beds for forty days, during which they were considered impure and were banned from church. My bedchamber adjoined the chapel, though, and I should have been able to follow the ceremony through my hagioscope. Yet all I saw that day was a sea of backs. Even the voices of the officiating priests had difficulty getting through that tapestry of bodies crammed together against the wall, and all I caught were muffled fragments. Not that it mattered. God had already allowed me to see the baptism in my mind, and I knew every detail.

In the chapel, the Lady of Montfaucon, very honored to be one of Elzéar's godmothers, held my child tightly to her breast. She had come at a moment's notice, without her husband, who was visiting his estates in Montbéliard and had not been informed in time. Lothaire was there too. Nobody paid any heed to my father's absence—confined to his bed by a nasty fever, according to his wife. What mattered was Elzéar. He screamed so much when Thierry II plunged him into the cold water of the font that I feared doubt might be cast on the whole pleasant little fairy tale. But since everyone had contributed to the story and had his share in the invention of the miracle, nobody would dream of reducing it to some tawdry episode. Only Douce, whom I knew to be skeptical, could have attempted a comment, but her words, had been held in check by the total conviction of the archbishop, who, in deciding to baptize my child himself and in helping me to choose godfathers and godmothers for him among the important people of the earldom, had so strangely involved himself in this madness. From this point onwards, truth would be meaningless. Everyone seemed to be carefully avoiding asking me the simple question that would have dispelled the mystery once and for all.

Elzéar was not given back to me immediately after his baptism. The Lady of Montfaucon clutched him for a long time to her heart, asserting that he felt well there and that, with a little luck, he would cure her of the sweats and hot flashes that had been causing her such discomfort recently. She laughed and talked a lot, determined to return often to the Whispers to teach the Credo, the Pater Noster, and the Ten Commandments to her beautiful godchild. "I'll give him a psalter, I'll show him images of the saints and explain to him how horrible Hell is by putting him in front of a cauldron full of boiling water. That was how my mother demonstrated the torments of the damned to me." For her, Elzéar was a kind of poultice, to be applied conscientiously over her whole body in order to make the most of its holy effect.

Many strangers now settled around Sainte-Agnès. Still pinned to his bed, my father was in no position to fight this proliferation of merchants, pilgrims, busy-bodies, and clerics who either wanted to see my son and converse with me, or were content to remain in the surroundings to take advantage of being there. It did not cross anyone's mind to ask me who Elzéar's father was or even how the boy had acquired his stigmata. They all told me their sorrows, confessed their greatest sins, implored me to intercede with Christ, the virgin, the angels, and the saints on behalf of some loved one still alive or some dead relative. They even tried sometimes, through me, to negotiate a little miracle with a too-distant God. I would smile at the folly of those who imagined they could resolve their temporal concerns in this way, but their faith was great, and I consented to do whatever I could, while trying to suggest simpler solutions.

Before long, I noticed that they mostly addressed my mutilated ear and leaned ostentatiously toward it when they spoke. My absent ear had the depth of a well: people threw into it everything they wanted God to know.

What interest would all these people have had in killing the goose that laid the golden egg? In doubting the woman from whom they expected so much?

Every morning, as soon as the gates of the precinct were opened, a few privileged people set up their stalls in the court-yard of the castle—no doubt they had paid money to the cap-

tain of the guards or of the steward for the right to install themselves as close as possible to my cell—while the other merchants remained outside the walls, at the foot of the fence.
Everyone tried to take advantage of this magnificent chaos,
and Douce, who was commanding the houschold during her
husband's illness, made no objection to anything. From noon
onwards, she allowed in unarmed visitors, merely demanding
that the courtyard be emptied of everyone, pilgrims and merchants, by vespers, so that the great gate could be closed. At
that time, the castle again became a private space for a few
hours, and those outside organized themselves as best they
could.

It was the beginning of spring, that period of the ycar when
an hour of daylight was the equivalent of an hour of night. The
hours in my century were somewhat elastic divisions. The days,
like the nights, always had twelve hours, in December as in
June. The duration of an hour of daylight was therefore three
times as long at the beginning of July as it was around
Christmas. The bells of the presbytery of Hautepierre, where a
monk was in charge of the time, imposed their rhythm on the
whole fiefdom. They struck the nine liturgical hours, calling
the faithful to prayer, and the bells of all the chapels in the
region replied in canon. Ivette was sleeping at the castle now,
and it was to her that I entrusted Elzéar between sext and vespers, so that he should become accustomed to the fresh air of
the outside world and not spend all his time in my cramped,
unhealthy cell.

Soon after the archbishop had gone, a merchant of relics
had established himself beneath the great maple. This red-
faced giant, who offered all kinds of remains of saints, greatly
amused me. He boasted of having some of my hair, as well as
a lock of St. Agnes's hair that changed color every day and that
never seemed to run out even though he sold most of it every
day. I saw him hand a pilgrim one of Christ's milk teeth in

return for a small but well-filled purse. He claimed to have a piece of the foreskin of the child Jesus, as well as an incredible chalk powder to be mixed with wine: "Milk of the Virgin," he would say, "which I gathered myself not far from Bethlehem in that white grotto where the mother of God once suckled her child." He had just added to his absurd collection a tattered piece of cloth in which Elzéar was supposed to have been wrapped at his birth, even though the actual square of cloth, bleached by Ivette and embroidered by me with a little prayer, was still intact around my son's body. The big man would become quite voluble as he held this wretched piece of material in his hand and bellowed that it was imbued with the scent of the holy child.

"A cloth you just have to rub over your wounds and they'll be healed. I also brought these splinters of the True Cross back from the Holy Land. Just leave them to infuse in hot water and they'll cure most incurable ailments. And here in this ebony casket is a very small bone of St. Peter, easy to carry on your travels, which yours truly was able to pluck from Rome!"

The name of this colossus was Martin. He resembled an enormous barrel, had not a single hair left on his head, and lied shamelessly, but his smile had such charm that it concealed his ugliness. He distributed it warmly to everyone and gave his listeners the feeling that they were important people. Addressing his customers as if he had always known them, this charlatan exuded sincerity, honesty, and good humor, and it was a real joy to see him hoodwinking everyone. From his neck hung lucky formulas that he offered pregnant women.

"Stories from the life of St. Margaret who managed to escape the belly of a dragon with the help of a small cross, stories that every pregnant woman should carry on her to make sure that she'll deliver the child as quickly as possible, that he won't perish, and that she herself won't die in childbirth!"

He often interrupted his speeches to swallow a piece of

cheese or bread, to animate a little articulated statue of the
Virgin, whose arms he could move with the help of two sticks,
or to address a compliment to Bérengère, like someone throwing seeds to a hen: "Here she is again, the prettiest girl in the
castle!" And Douce's maidservant would take pleasure in passing him again and again to hear his praises. They teased each
other constantly. She would chuckle as she looked at his smiling face, become intoxicated with his fine words, and as soon
as she was within his reach, he would take advantage to fondle
her heavy breasts a little or tenderly pinch her buttocks right at
the birth of the thigh, just two fingers from her sexual parts.

Until this character arrived, I had never noticed how beautiful Bérengère was. I had always thought her stern and grace-
less, but now, suddenly glorified by this rogue's attentions, her
huge curves began to undulate beneath her green skirts, and
she would wiggle her hips and arch her back and flash her
eyes. She seemed to draw so much pleasure from all that, it
mattered little to her that the two of them were making the
whole household gossip. In Martin's presence, Bérengère
became herself.

I loved to watch their amorous dance, to see big, heavy
Bérengère so light in the palms of his hands, to sense the simple joy they had in looking at each other, in standing close to
each other, in brushing against each other, in rubbing each
other in passing as if nothing had happened, in modifying their
posture—swelling their chests like birds, pulling their stom-
achs in, combing their eyebrows with their fingertips, moisten-
ing their lips. And the nicest thing of all was to hear the loud
pealing of their laughter.

Gradually, without my even noticing, my attention moved
away from the hagioscope to my son and all the people he
attracted. God occupied me less than his creatures from now
on, and I never grew tired of watching them, listening to them,

trying to understand what motivated their little brains. I no longer dreaded their judgment, or even that of God. I had not lied, I had merely kept silent about a truth that nobody wanted to hear anyway, and my silence had offered a blank space to be embroidered, an emptiness that everyone had seized on with delight. Even my confessor, my brother Benoît, chose carefully from his penitential the questions to ask me through the window of my cell.

S ome days after Elzéar's baptism, Douce came back to see
me at night, before vigils. She scratched again at my
shutter. The light of an enormous moon rained down on
the maple and on my young stepmother's chalky features, leaving her eyes black in the shadow of her lashes.

"How's my father?"

"So weak now, he can only moan. He's fading away. For six
days, I've been calming him thanks to Bérengère's remedies, I
keep him quiet with drugs but am unable to restore his sanity."

"Hasn't anyone tried to see him?"

"I've learned how to scare away our people. My threats have
kept the household at a distance. Only your brother Benoît
insists a little, but the birth of your son, the arrival of the archbishop, the preparations for Easter, and the constant passing of
pilgrims have so captured his attention that he doesn't see the
time drift by. I've forbidden anyone to enter the nuptial chamber and I always keep it locked. All the bustle has distracted
the servants and I've been able to use that. Have no fear, I
alone can hear your father's ramblings. And believe me, I'd
prefer to find a way to silence them forever. I regret speaking
so harshly to you during our first interview. My ignorance led
me to believe that you had crucified your baby in an attempt
to make everyone forget your sin."

"Did you think me so wicked?"

"Forgive me. Thanks to my husband's delirium, I now
know much more both about you and about him. But you see,

I haven't come only to make you this confession. We're linked by the same secret, our destinies are intertwined, and I've realized it's you alone that I can trust. So you must listen to me and believe me in your turn!"

"Don't be so mysterious. Just tell me!"

"When I awoke earlier, I saw that your father's other hand had been nailed to the bed. And yet the door was closed from inside, I myself had drawn the bolt. Nobody could have entered while I slept. Nobody! I'm really afraid, Esclarmonde. Do you think the dead could be responsible?"

"The dead? Why the dead?"

"Ever since I started sleeping on a straw mattress in a corner of our chamber for fear of sharing your father's bed, I've been hearing whispers during my sleep. Someone is scratching and moaning in the thickness of the walls. I hear a woman's voice, already long dead. My Bérengère has questioned the servants, everyone has told her the same story. The name of the woman whose words the stones sometimes let through is Emengarde. She was buried alive in the foundations and the big tower was built over her body by my husband's grandfather, Achard."

"Everyone around here knows that legend. It is because of her that the fiefdom is called the Whispers, but I've never heard of the castle walls weeping."

"For several nights now, Emengarde's moans have mingled with your father's. I'm certain it was her ghost that put in that second nail."

Douce lifted her hands to her face. In wiping away her tears, she spread shadows all around her eyes. The passage of her dirty fingers left long dark streaks on her skin.

"Is it true you are afraid of the night?" I asked.

"Not of the night, of sleep."

"It is said that you force Bérengère to lie across your door."

"She does that, but I don't force her. She understood that it reassures me."

"And from what does your maidservant hope to protect you?"

"I sometimes walk while I'm asleep. In truth, the only thing I'm afraid of is myself."

"Show me your hands!"

Douce came as close as possible to the wall and put her hands through the bars. I placed them under my candle. Her fingers were stained with blood and it was that dried blood that, mixed with her tears, was now trickling down her cheeks.

"Did you touch your husband's wounds when you awoke?"

"No. The night is so bright that I was able to see your father crucified from my straw mattress. I lay there for a moment, unable to move, then summoned up the courage to come here."

"Then I don't think the dead have anything to do with it!"

Douce looked at her hands in her turn. "Do you think I myself nailed him to his bed while I slept?"

"You are torn between hate and love! You can no longer protect him. If he stays nailed to the nuptial bed like that, he will die within a few days despite your friend's medicines, and perhaps he will even die by your hands while you are asleep. If you want to remain at the Whispers, you must tell him what I told you during our first interview. Tell him that Esclarmonde wants him to prepare for the Crusade. Have no fear. My elder brother, Guillaume, will follow his father, he is passionate and avid for adventure, and his wife lacks character and won't have the strength to keep him here. Jean, his younger brother, always follows wherever he goes, so he will leave too. Benoît won't leave his order, and as for Benjamin, he is not yet of age to command a household. My father will therefore leave you in charge of the fiefdom. He will ask the archbishop to let you be its mistress during his absence. If you bear a son, whatever happens to your husband you will remain at the castle for a long time still and nobody will try to marry you off again. If they do, I will use my new found power and demand that you be allowed to stay by my side and help me with Elzéar. Let your husband go and redeem himself!"

"I'll repeat to him, word for word, what you told me six days ago. But I don't know if he'll have the strength to hear me."

"Do it as soon as possible, but before you do, wash your face and hands. If he sees you by the light of a torch with all that blood on you, he might think you had just murdered someone."

My stepmother had not moved. She seemed lost in thought, as if she could not make up her mind to bring our discussion to a close.

"The part of me that escapes my understanding," she murmured at last, as if to herself, "the things I do when I am asleep, belong so little to me that I'll never know who crucified my husband, whether it was I or the ghost of Emengarde!"

"The important thing is that this act has helped you to submit to the will of God. How do you propose to go about taking out those nails?"

"Bérengère will help me. She has the strength of a man, and she knows what your father has been through, I haven't hidden his condition from her. In fact, I've never hidden anything from her, apart from what your father's ramblings have told me about Elzéar. It is she who helps me care for my husband. But the wench wasn't lying in front of her master's chamber last night, protecting my sleep. She took advantage of the moonlight to go gallivanting off. Nothing scares her. Of course, a woman built like her can defend herself against any devil. I suppose she met that awful vendor of relics somewhere in the woods and won't return until morning. It's scarcely believable, but she's become madly infatuated with that fat charlatan."

"Yes, I've seen her with Martin. They're well matched. I hadn't thought she was so pleasing."

"It's just that sleeping like that outside my door whenever I take a husband, she's exposed herself to all those who grope for girls at night, and I fully believe that, having offered herself so often in the dark, she's acquired a taste for caresses. The more she ripens, the less restrained she is. By day, she pretends to be stern, for she cares about her reputation, but her virtue is only a façade. She says she's already tarnished, so one more blemish won't matter. In her eyes, this is all nothing but a minor sin that will burn very quickly in the fires of Purgatory."

"What does she do not to bear a child?"

"My mother found Bérengère on the banks of the Loue. She was no more than two and wore nothing but a meager green shift. Nobody ever found out where she came from. Doubtless she had been abandoned there by some vagabond. Out of charity, she was raised with me. For a long time, she turned her back on the world of men and spoke only to the trees and stones. And then, little by little, the little savage became attached to me. We were inseparable, and over the years I saw her amass her incredible knowledge about plants. Wherever she goes, she questions the elders, collects their recipes, and gathers seeds. She knows all the secrets of the flowers, and knows what to do not to become pregnant. She often says that she has acquired nothing on this earth but that knowledge, my friendship, and the two green robes I sewed for her, and that's not enough to bring up a child. She refuses to bring a child into the world and entrust it to the agitated waters of this century in a little cradle."

"I shall pray for her."

"She'll be back in the morning and then we'll remove the nails from your father's hands. He's so weak, he won't be able to stop us."

The courtyard echoed with the sound of horses' hooves. The great gate had been opened earlier than usual to let my father out. A mere twelve days after Bérengère had removed the nails from him, he could already mount his palfrey and hold it with reins taut, despite the pain in his hands. After matins, Douce had smeared his wounds with a lily-based ointment and carefully bandaged his palms, and then his wounded hands had found peace on her breasts. Since he had recovered his senses, my father had rediscovered his taste for caresses and, although this was a day of abstinence, he wanted to enjoy his wife as much as possible before leaving for the Crusade. Knowing that his sins would soon be redeemed, he did not worry about following the rules of continence imposed by the Church. Besides, there were so many days of abstinence that everyone ended up ignoring them, in spite of pressure from their confessors.

On that first Wednesday after Easter, the Lord of the Whispers had left his wife's bed early to set off for Besançon to see Prince-Archbishop Thierry II, whose permission he needed to join the Holy Roman Emperor, Frederick Barbarossa, then count of Burgundy, in his crusade to liberate Jerusalem.

My father did not feel comfortable in town, he felt oppressed as soon as he had crossed the Pont Battant. Entering that bend of the River Doubs into which men had piled to make a city and making his way through the mire of the alleys between the tall houses with their narrow gables filled him with dread. He preferred to stay on his horse and look down on that restless, noisy mass of people. Around his nervous mount the activity went on: garbage emptied in the street, vendors selling tripe and fritters, pigs and goats led on foot to market, barrels being rolled, bundles of sticks being carried, sheep having their throats cut, there was begging, stealing, defecating, all happening at the same time, in the same hubbub. Lent was over and trade had started up again with renewed vigor since the end of the fast.

My father wondered how so many bodies could keep together in such a small space, breathing the same pestilential air, screaming incomprehensibly at each other, mixing legs and heads and arms and voices, gathering around his charger, which had to push them with its breast to keep moving forward. This world of merchants made him feel as if he were under attack, he hated its dark, swarming hive. In the town, everybody had something to sell and he was hailed on all sides. Even the young women of the poor, who had nothing to offer but their own bodies, called to him, made faces to him on the dark thresholds of houses.

The cathedral of Saint-Jean rose beyond the Porte Noire.

Seeing its colossal form from the foot of Mont Saint-Étienne, my father, who admired it as a building, was always surprised that such a flower of stone had grown there, that such splendor could have been born amid all that agitation. And yet there was no doubt, cathedrals were the children of the cities, serene emanations of that urban squalor—and of the gold from their commerce. They majestically crowned the rising power of the cities.

The Lord of the Whispers did not dismount until he reached the courtyard of the archbishop's palace. His feet had not trodden the fetid ground of the town, only his horse had walked in its mud. He was immediately received by his liege lord, who declared himself delighted to see him in better health and very impatient to learn what had brought him to Besançon.

The pontiff listened attentively to what I had ordered and, when my father fell silent, he appeared surprised.

"Is that all?"

"Yes, my lord," said my father.

"The emperor is preparing to retake Jerusalem from the infidel, it is only right that you join him. The kings of England and France haven't advanced so far in their plans, but a great assembly is due to be held at Vézelay this summer, and they will no doubt meet up with the army of the Holy Roman Empire on the way. But didn't your daughter say anything about me?"

"Only that I was to ask for your blessing."

"I'm surprised she did not demand that I follow you on that tremendous journey."

"Your Excellency, one cannot demand anything of such a great man as you!"

Then, without warning, the archbishop's fury erupted with all the violence of a summer storm.

"You don't dare repeat to me your daughter's exact words, is that it?" he boomed. "You don't have her courage. She asked you to accompany me to the Holy Land, and you, O man of little faith, are afraid to be the messenger of God. How dare you fear me more than you fear His power? Many men of the Church will travel by your side, many men of great ability! Princes, minor lords, knights, foot soldiers, priests, or archbishops, we will march side by side, sharing the same faith, and we will take back Christ's tomb as much by prayer as by arms. I cannot possibly remain in this palace if God wants me at the foot of the Holy City. You tremble at the idea of telling me the truth, but I know that young girl is close to the Almighty and I hear the order you did not dare formulate. I have looked into her child's wounds as if through a window. We will fight the Crusade together, by the emperor's side, and perhaps you will prove more courageous in combat than you are in my court-yard!"

The archbishop was shouting so loudly, waving his long, thin arms in all directions, that Father thought he was going to beat him. He knew it was not possible to contradict such a per-sonage, and he waited patiently for the stream of words to run dry. Douce had told him nothing concerning Thierry II, he was completely unaware of the will of God in all this, but he did not refute anything. The archbishop was a man, and perhaps he, too, had some mortal sin to atone for. The pontiff's black eyes were like burning coals in his thin, pointed face. Without raising his head, my father asked his lord for permission to entrust his fiefdom to his wife Douce. The archbishop, who in his rage had risen from his chair and was about to leave the great hall, consented to this, but his thoughts had already set off on their journey.

And yet, as he was just about to pass through the majestic oak door reinforced with embossed brass that led to his apart-ments, he suddenly stopped and dismissed his entourage in order to talk for a moment to my father man to man. His anger had receded as if blown away.

"Take care not to empty the coffers of your fiefdom in order to arm your men, and don't leave Esclarmonde defenseless in your Castle of Whispers. God alone knows how long a holy war will last. I wouldn't like any misfortune to befall your daughter and her miraculous child in our absence. For my part, I'll give the necessary instructions to make sure they are both protected by the chapter of Saint-Jean. The dean of the church of Saint-Étienne, who has been contesting our status as mother church for so long, would use any means at his disposal to assert his power. He might take advantage of my throne being vacant to try to weaken me. Your family is precious to me, I have made adventurous choices concerning it. What can I do, I love nice stories! Christ was a great storyteller, His parables are jewels. The strength of the Church lies also in the stories that have come down through the centuries and in our ability to still create wonderful fables in the service of the faith. But I know that our time loves to find culprits, and I wouldn't like anyone to call your daughter a heretic once I am no longer there. For it's possible, my friend, that we shan't return to this earldom. If God has decided to make you the companion of my last hours, I hope He will give you back your tongue and spare me your courtier's cowardice."

The day after this interview, my father set off again and rode directly from Besançon to the castle of Montfaucon to speak with Lothaire's father. Having heard the archbishop's anxieties, he needed to find a way to finance his departure without leaving his wife, his daughter, and those two infants he would leave behind in a state of destitution.

Montfaucon was on his guard at first, fearing that I was forcing him, too, to set off for Palestine to wage war. He had made that journey before, and had no desire to again sweat blood and water in the Holy Land. He was getting older and these days preferred hunting to fighting. Once reassured that he was not directly involved in this whole business, he warmly invited my father to dinner and was surprised to see that both his hands were bandaged. In the hubbub of the great hall, where the table had been raised on trestles, he leaned toward the Lord of the Whispers, whom he had seated at his left, as close as possible to the fireplace, and said, "Don't tell me you, too, bear stigmata! It's a mania in your family! Do you make holes in your hands to attract attention? If my memory serves me well, your father also had a hand pierced by a lance during a tournament. Since my return, my wife has been endlessly telling me about this miraculous child whose godmother she is and who has cured her of her sweats. She's trying to encourage me to follow my brother Thierry and you into this holy war, I'm sure of it, because she wants this house for herself. You'll have to tell her your daughter didn't mention me—or, rather, no, tell her that the Almighty needs me here, on my lands, to protect her dear godson. Are you going to yield your fiefdom to your eldest son?"

"No, my sons are leaving with me. I would also like to take Benjamin, who is a squire in your house."

"Do you intend to involve him in this adventure, too?"

"He's only eleven, so he wouldn't fight, but I'm determined to have him with us on the journey. It's an experience I'd have loved to have had with my father. Only Benoît will remain in his priory. The archbishop has consented for me to leave the management of my lands to Douce and has assured me that nobody will touch my fiefdom or my family for as long as we are away."

"So your wife's going to be mistress of the Whispers! That'll only make mine even madder that she is. Try not to get yourself killed, my friend! I'll give you thirty men. With yours, that'll make forty knights, not to mention my brother's foot soldiers. I'll contribute to the upkeep of your little army. I feel much too old to launch into such a venture with you, but if I can't sacrifice my life I'll at least invest a little of my fortune in it. My fourth son, Amey, will go with you. Ever since Amaury de Joux married his beautiful Berthe, he's been anxious to leave the earldom. He'll bear my colors and my wife will have to be content with that! As for my brother, he'll finally be able to try out his famous machines, I suspect that's his main reason for going. You have no idea of the man's mechanical genius, or of his obstinacy. He'll strip ships of their masts to make battering rams, and their pulleys and ropes to equip his siege engines. Nothing could better correspond to his dream than the siege of Jerusalem."

For a time, the two men stopped talking about the journey and the conversation turned to the cooking of carp, which they both liked quite soft, and to the delicious heat of the long peppers with which the cook at Montfaucon copiously seasoned his dishes.

"If you could take Lothaire, too," Montfaucon finally said, "that would be glad tidings indeed! The filthy beast does just what he wants! He has never recovered from having missed his wedding. Your daughter cut short his manhood, and now he's lost interest in both wenches and arms and bores me rigid with his music. Let him leave with his vielle, his songs, and the mad love he has for that witch Esclarmonde! Where does my son get this unfortunate tendency to love more than is acceptable?"

"If he wants to follow me, he has his place."

Side by side, at the high end of the big table, the two lords shared cups and trenchers—those thick slices of stale bread used as plates—and speared the best pieces of food with the points of their knives. They had known each other forever. Their fathers and grandfathers had traveled to Jerusalem together. This time, one of the sons would leave alone, already weakened by the years.

The next day, having slept on one of the straw mattresses in the big hall where they had dined, my father took his leave and as soon as prime was over set off on the road to his lands. He wanted to join his wife as soon as possible, drown in her bed, intoxicate himself with her scent.

M y father started to worry about the sun once the fires of Saint-Jean were extinguished.

After pushing the merchants out of the castle precincts and regulating the flow of pilgrims, though without forbidding them access to the chapel, the Lord of the Whispers had carefully prepared for his departure, initiating Douce into the management of the estate, divesting himself of his functions one by one, stripping himself of his power, gradually erasing himself from the household and watching it live without his orders. Little by little, he had even stopped hunting and caressing his wife's round belly—too round now, and inhabited by another. He was getting ready to disappear, and thought only of the sun and of that land without shadow that was called holy.

I was told that he spent his absent hours sitting under the trees on the edge of the fields watching his peasants hard at work with their scythes or billhooks in their hands, their feet stuck in that good earth of the Whispers—which was already no longer his—brought low by the long hours of July, exhausted by the haymaking, then by the harvest, the flailing, and the picking. I imagined him in the shade of a lime tree or an oak watching them laboring all day long in the burning sun, singing as they worked, for never within living memory had anyone seen such fine harvests or such grains of corn, grains as big as the holes in the hands of the holy child. And the newly cleared land had yielded almost as much as the rest of the domain. In spite of their fatigue, their hearts were jubilant—

nobody would be hungry that winter, and they would face the cold without anxiety. My father could leave with his mind at rest. The granaries were full and his grateful people would venerate his name as much as those of his holy daughter and his little angel. Ever since Elzéar's birth and the master's decision to leave for the Crusade, the sky had been clement, the sun generous, and the earth fertile.

Everyone remembered the difficult times they had known before Esclarmonde had sacrificed herself for them, before she had chosen to offer her life to God. For two years running, the corn, rye, and vines had been ruined by storms and frost, and the harvests had rotted uncut. The land was so soaked, they were unable to trace furrows for planting seeds, and there had been hardly any rain in the fiefdom of the Whispers. The children, above all, had fallen like flies. The poor had seen their arms and legs blacken and come loose from their trunks like dead branches. Not to mention all those times when they had had to support my father in his quarrels, to give ever more so that he could go off and wage war on one of his neighbors, and to contemplate the fields laid waste by the passing of soldiers.

The world had changed and the strength of the old formulas had been exhausted. The incantations chanted to the bread, the stones, and the fountains, the little girls left naked and walking as if in procession over the frozen land so that the corn should rise better—all that old magic of the calends of January, which the priests pursued in the confessional, now proved to have no effect. Oh, yes, the poor people had suffered much until their virgin had interceded on their behalf and calmed the wrath of Heaven. And she had done more than calm it. She had put Death to sleep.

The serfs had noticed nothing at first, but it was a fact that nobody had died in the fiefdom since Esclarmonde had gone into her tomb and, of all these miracles, that seemed the most remarkable. Yes, nobody was dying now at the Whispers. Women in labor, babies, old people, everyone in the region, even the frailest, seemed to have been spared by the Grim Reaper since the bell of Sainte-Agnès had rung for the first time. Some asserted that Death had been too curious and had naively allowed himself to be trapped with me in my little cell the day I was put in the tomb.

At the end of August, the rosebush planted by Lothaire beside my window gave me the scent of its very first flower, Douce gave birth to a big boy whom my father named Phébus, and Thierry II decided on the date of departure. The Lord of the Whispers would leave us one week after his wife had returned to the world after her period of impurity.

I was hoping that my father would talk with me for a few moments before setting off. He had never again appeared outside my window since the day he had returned Elzéar to me with pierced hands.

He came on the eve of his departure, laden with heavy silence, and I did not think that either of us would be able to break that silence. But my father broke it, like a man breaking bread. He spoke to me of the sun, and I sensed that he was telling me of his coming death, that he was offering me his head as a final tribute.

"When my father returned from the Crusade," he said, "he told me that in the East the sun kills more knights than even the arrows of the infidel."

"Then cover your helmet with a veil of cloth in order not to boil inside it, and wear a shirt of mail or a tunic of boiled leather rather than your long coat of mail, which would weigh you down too much."

We talked thus about his kit, the route he would take to join the emperor, the knights who would ride with him, those they would find again on the way.

"Amaury de Joux and Amey de Montfaucon are both com-ing. They hate each other so much because of Berthe that the journey promises to be a lively one. But Lothaire won't be with us. He refuses to leave the woman to whom his heart is attached. His father is convinced that in rejecting him you have neutered him."

"It seems to me the only thing I cut off was my ear."

"I'm not joking, Esclarmonde. Montfaucon doesn't dare say so, but he hates you so much that, if he had the power, he wouldn't hesitate to have you burned alive. He says you are a witch and have drowned his son's manhood. Watch him like the plague. You robbed him of his best hunting companion. Lothaire has stopped running after both girls and stags. He's become besotted with a minstrel who's teaching him the vielle, and he writes poems that he sets to music."

"And which he often comes to sing to me."

"I know. The archbishop has also paid you several visits. Is he convinced that it's you who are making him go on the Crusade?"

"He was. But we've talked about it and now he accepts that he alone decided on this journey, that I made no attempt to force him, and that you weren't delivering any message to him from me when you went to Besançon."

"Does he bear me a grudge for not having refuted him?"

"No. He's happy to go with you."

"I was neither a coward nor a liar before he called me so. I only became so afterwards, when I could found no answer to his accusations. I'm leaving with a vain man who thinks he can bend events to his convenience. He isn't driven by faith, but by his own madness. Did you know that he spends his time imagining engines of war? Why have you not detained him here? He's a powerful protector for you and Elzéar. He fears that his enemies will attack you in his absence, that they may even call you a heretic. It would be more judicious to keep him within reach."

"My father, you misunderstand my intentions. I'm not trying to deceive anyone. If men go astray, it's in spite of me. Let Thierry II go wherever he sees fit! It's true that I didn't have the heart to sacrifice my son to your sin and that I said nothing concerning you. My silence is meager armor, but it is the only armor I was able to take with me into my tomb. It would only take one question to tear that light veil, and if that arrow should be fired one day, you can rest assured I shan't lie. A lie is too heavy a burden to bear for one who chooses to live so close to the divine light."

"Will you ever be able to forgive a father who loved you so much in his folly? You who offered me the cross as a last hope of salvation, would you consent to sew this crucifix on my tunic?"

My father handed me four large strips of red cloth and the broad white sleeveless shift that he would wear over his shirt of mail.

I immediately set to work, and, as my needle attached his cross, my father sat silently, back stooped and legs parted, on the bench by the window that had been placed there for visitors. People passed by without even looking at him as he held his head in his hands, weighed down by the trial to come. Nobody paid him any heed. He had succeeded in making himself invisible.

"The sun haunts me. Even my nights are full of it. I know, my daughter, that we will never see each other again."

"The archbishop is leaving with his head filled with the engines of war that he has imagined, Emperor Frederick's one thought, it appears, is to avoid water, and you are obsessed by the bite of the sun. One does not leave a world without anxiety or without a dream."

"Thierry says that he has seen us in your son's hands, that his stigmata are windows."

"I myself have seen nothing in them but pain."

"Am I not ridiculous? In a fit of anger, like a brute, I pierced that child's hands and yet even I, knowing the truth, would like to believe in miracles and see in those marks a sign from God. I would so much like to ignore my own violence, my own sins, that I delude myself with nonsense. I sometimes catch myself forgetting who the child's father is. His beauty is the beauty of sin. But I alone know it for what it is."

"There, your cross is sewed on your tunic."

"You know, Montfaucon reminded me of something strange. My father also had a mark on his palm. He got it in a tournament."

"Go with a quiet mind, your daughter has forgiven you. And if God refuses you entry into His kingdom, I will find the words to oblige Him to open His door. We shall meet again in His light. Do not fear that sun!"

"Let me hug Elzéar for a moment, that I may measure the weight of my sin."

Elzéar was growing, but my father had organized our existence at the Whispers so well before leaving for the Crusade that it seemed to me sometimes as if that life could last forever.

The merchants no longer distracted me from my task since access to the castle courtyard had been forbidden them. But I missed fat Martin and his hodgepodge of relics. When it came to laughter, I now had to content myself with that of Bérengère, whose vast beauty seemed to increase with every passing day.

Every evening, in a few strides, she would reach the forest and there join her suitor, whose caresses had done so much to take the edge off her rigidity. At night, her cries of love spread through the woods, mingling in autumn with the languorous belling of the stags and sometimes even the howling of wolves. Toward the end of spring, the lovers moved to a different bed: the banks of the Loue. All summer long, the young giantess would moan while the waters murmured, so that woman and river, lying side by side beneath the clouds, seemed to be reaching the height of pleasure at the same time, and malicious gossips began accusing that pair of ogres of filling the night with seed. Yes, according to Ivette, that terrible man's semen had impregnated the Loue, and soon its green waters would be swarming with monsters!

As for Bérengère, she was surprised at the power she had acquired over men since she had let herself be kneaded thus by

Martin's big hands. It was as if their clandestine lovemaking had made her infinitely desirable.

During the day, all the young men of the household were at her heels, their eyes glued to her everlasting green skirts, shouting vulgar compliments at her, trying to touch her skin and caress her long golden locks, and she would chase them away like flies, but like flies they would immediately return to pester her.

She would mock the weakness of what was considered the stronger sex—how strong could they be, when a mere glance from her sufficed to lay them flat?—and laugh at such vanity. She herself never tired of her own body, whose charms she had discovered through Martin's eyes. At last she was able to display the natural grace of her gestures, a grace she had hitherto repressed, doubtless more out of caution than out of modesty. She had broken the invisible chains that had fettered her since childhood, that reserve that had been imposed on her, and she now gave herself up to the caress of the wind, the coolness of the undergrowth, the warmth of the sun. She would sometimes feel a sensual pleasure from the landscape or even a little breeze that lifted her skirts, as if she were coupling with the world for the brief moment that current of air lasted. Her round body shook as she moved, a constant spur to love, just like that joy that the desires of those who harassed her could never stifle, that joy that she herself could not contain, which flowed out of her, finding its outlet by day in laughter, and by night in those wonderful cries that set the castle aflame and fixed themselves in men's hearts like arrows.

Only Lothaire, who continued to lay siege to me in music, seemed insensitive to Bérengère's charms.

He had practiced hard, his voice had become smoother, and his poems were now so moving that I at last began to delight in them. When his vielle fell silent, we would sit there, facing one another, not speaking, and our eyes, like caged birds, could not stay in place, as if afraid to meet, afraid that if they did, they would be unable to extricate themselves. Our long silences were a delicious torture. Each of his visits was more painful than the last, and yet I was impatient for them.

His rosebush bore ever more flowers, and their voluptuous scent forced open my shutter, entered my cell, slid into my nose and mouth and over my lips and tongue and into my soul without my being able to shield myself from it.

But Elzéar was growing, and although he had not abandoned my breast, he now ate pap consisting of chicken or veal bouillon, soft-boiled eggs, chicken and rabbit cut into very small pieces—all things I remembered being fed as a child. As I was determined to give him his meals myself, wonderful aromas tickled my nostrils every day. I took such pleasure in watching my child tasting the food with his lips first and discovering a new flavor, before opening his mouth wide and stamping his little feet impatiently between each mouthful! I shared his sensations, the sweetness of apples baked with sugar or cinnamon-flavored blancmange, the texture of the mashed vegetables seasoned with verjuice and delightfully colored by saffron. His meals revived in me a range of tastes from which my gray reclusion had cut me off.

Was it a sin to gorge myself thus in thought? To immerse myself in aromas and flavors—and in Lothaire's songs, too? To listen to Bérengère's cries as she lay somewhere out there in the countryside?

Elzéar was growing, and even though I was relieved of him during those hours of the afternoon when the pilgrims were allowed to speak to me, he demanded more and more of my attention. In order not to fail in my religious task, and to serve as best I could those who implored my help, I cut down on my sleep, and spent my nights in prayer. I wished I could have withstood exhaustion even better. I wished I would never again have to close my eyes, because the moments when I abandoned myself caused me so much anguish. Yes, I would have preferred not to sleep at all, in order to spare myself the visions that overwhelmed me as soon as my vigilance was relaxed.

I was not trying to punish myself by depriving myself of sleep. I have never appreciated excess, nor did I dream of following the example of some of my sisters, of whom it was said that they washed the wounds of wretched lepers and then drank the water with the foul scabs still floating in it. I remained moderate in all things, content during this period to advise, to read minds, and to give hope, making use of that incredible network of anchoresses and Bérengère's talents as an herbalist. My position gave such force to my words that strangers obeyed them and found they were helped by them. Thanks to me, they were able to bear their sufferings, redeem their sins, recover their faith. Sick people said they had been cured, but what part did I play in these miracles? Even Ivette was telling all and sundry that by laying hands on her I had freed her from some mysterious ailment, that a single caress from me had sufficed to obliterate the pustules that had been growing on her side!

I did not think I had performed real miracles, but I could not deny that Death had abdicated. The local people were still not dying. Nobody had expired in the domain of the Whispers and, apart from a few strangers, nobody had been buried there since the beginning of my reclusion. And that was what I could not understand.

My son prevented me from becoming too intoxicated with this strange hold that I had over people. I could have asked them for anything in return for the remission of their sins, and, although I was careful not to wield this power, it was nevertheless dangerously exciting. I was responsible for their souls.

Unaware of the strength my position had given me, Lothaire was trying through his songs to bring down the walls of my cell.

Elzéar was growing. For the moment he was still able to slip between the bars of my window, and, as his head was now getting bigger at a slower rate than before, it was impossible to say how much time we still had to be happy together.

Now that he had started walking, he often strolled naked beneath his red shirt. On days of fine weather, he spent long hours with Phébus in the shade of the lime trees in the ornamental garden, or beneath the blue ceilings of the castle, still closely watched by the women, but as soon as the bells rang for vespers he would return to my enclosing arms and sleep every night on the straw in my cell.

His little heart beating fast beneath his warm flesh, he would breathe his intense love into my neck, and I would tremble at the thought that soon I would have to deprive myself of his fingers tangled in my hair, of his gentleness, of his warmth. His skin smelled of the outside world, the wind in the great trees, the newly cut grass, the lilacs, and his breath filled my tomb with the scent of honey and fruit. He would tenderly rub his cheek or his blond hair—so full of sunlight—against my thin shoulder. Every day, in addition to those scents he would collect on his body, like a bee, he would give me a flower, a leaf, or a pretty stone gathered outside and I would marvel at it. I would sometimes become quite engrossed in these gifts of his: we just have to look at something for a very long time for a door to open and draw us in.

Jehanne's mother, who, slowed down by age as she was, only rarely came to the castle, would tell me as often as she could that I had to prepare myself, that the time would come soon enough, and that I had already been lucky to conceive such a delicate boy with such a small head.

"None of mine could have slipped between these bars for

so long," she would say with a smile. "Look, Phébus is already taller than him. Of course, he has quite a nurse. A strapping lass your father brought from the forest of Chaux."

Douce had only a little time to devote to her child. She worked ceaselessly, and with the help of her steward became an excellent administrator of the fiefdom. We talked every day, but never about that inevitable separation, and I sensed that she did not dare say anything to me about it, so aware was she of how painful it would be for me to be parted from Elzéar. I would tell her of my nocturnal visions, and she would confide her anxieties, which she could no longer tell anyone about since love had stolen her Bérengère from her and she had become the sole mistress of the Whispers. To the others, Douce only spoke to give orders, she left nothing to chance and would allow no weakness. Nobody would have dared steal, or even answer her back. The only thing sweet about her these days was her name. I was the one person allowed to criticize her authority.

It seemed to me sometimes that the Whispers had freed itself from the power of men once and for all, and that Bérengère, Douce, and I now held the threads of the world, each in her domain, that we could move people about as we wished, just as Martin animated his articulated little Virgin.

For Elzéar, the cell was like a part of his mother's body. Nothing ever equaled the force of his gaze resting on me, that desire for absolute love, that hold he had over me, and I savored the immense pleasure of gratifying him with my mere presence. Although he had emerged from my flesh, he was no longer me, but he remained connected to me by invisible threads and let me share his sensations and guide his first steps. The walls that contained me were a stone bosom, a place impregnated with my voice and my smell, which he left every day as if freeing himself from an embrace. At first, our daily separations had been a wrench: he would scream and grip the bars with all the strength in his little body, and his tiny fingers had to be pried away from them one by one, while I held back my tears and thought of the day when he would be gone forever. What a pang in my soul!

As he grew, he no longer feared to go away. He would kiss me one last time and cling to my breast, then pass from my arms to Ivette's. He knew that his mother would not be going anywhere, and so he no longer dreaded these departures. What a strange experience it is to learn thus to live for oneself! My son was exploring a world that was forbidden to me. My son was detaching himself from me, safe in the knowledge that he would always find me where he had left me, sealed within the stone walls of my chapel.

This feeling of being wrenched from him churned my innards every day, and every time my child and his smiling face disappeared from my field of vision, it seemed as if he were leaving for the ends of the earth, leaving me alone in that cell, alone with my madness. Without him, how long the time was!

We had invented a little ritual for when we were reunited: as soon as he was back in my space, he loved to sit down on my lap and stroke my face for a long time. He had done so before uttering his first words, before he could walk, he had done so as soon as he had acquired control of his hands, and he continued to repeat those same gestures every time he came back into my arms. He would encircle my hollow cheeks in his pierced little palms and run his hands over my features, playing at distorting them, kneading my thin face. Sometime he would obliterate my mouth or my one ear by covering them with all his fingers, sometimes he would hide my eyes and laugh to see them disappear. By molding my face, he ended up burying my eyeballs so deeply in their sockets that he would turn my gaze inward, and, in the white imprint of his fingers, I would be aware of fleeting images, the remnants of which would veil my sight long after his little hands had withdrawn. These bodies floated in the air, unconnected to the world, bright filaments in the darkness of my cell, black patches in the light from outside.

Elzéar was imposing images on me.

He would introduce them into my eyes and these fragments would hide behind my eyelids and remain in my head until nightfall. During my sleep, these specks would unfold into landscapes, and as they grew brighter they would reveal to me what my father was seeing, had seen, or would see under the sun. Images appeared to me, incomplete at first, but then developing into visions so precise that I could no longer doubt their reality.

In my child's hands, I saw the endless cohort of Crusaders rolling eastward, I saw a hundred thousand men marching behind Emperor Frederick Barbarossa, and I became aware of my father's astonishment and anxiety as he rode with his sons in that stream of warriors and caparisoned horses.

As Elzéar gradually developed more dexterity with words, with things, with his body, my father was plunging further eastward.

A vast road unfurled before me at night in my cell. I felt my father's fatigue in my own body and, at the end of my arms, the weight of his sword as it ravaged Thrace. I heard the voice of Thierry II intoning his prayers and, on that ever-receding horizon, I would watch for the morning sun, wondering each time if this would be the one that would finish off my father, but every evening the sun would fall without having stabbed him. The days followed one another, the lands and the cities, the kingdom of Hungary, the Byzantine empire, and Adrianople, the sacking of which had opened to them the gates of the Bosporus, and the sermons of Thierry II galvanized the troops of the Almighty, using the Bible to justify the blood spilled—a necessary evil, he would tell the warriors, just as it had been necessary to sacrifice the firstborn of Egypt to reach the Holy Land.

During the crossing of the strait, I read in the eyes of emperor, to whom my father had gradually grown closer, the same terror he had already manifested during the crossing of the Danube, that fear that gripped him every time he was handed a container full of water. The reflection of his panic would sway on the surface of the liquid, and his eyes, bulging with that twofold shudder, terrified him so much that, attempting to conceal his panic with a fit of temper, he would violently reject the water and demand wine. But his companions, startled by the great Frederick Barbarossa's sudden aversion to an element most other people welcomed, were not fooled. It was whispered in the ranks that the emperor feared the water in his gold goblet as if there were a danger it would rise up, seize him by the throat, and prevent him from reaching the Holy Land. Everyone was surprised, thinking that God alone knew why the old man, considered to be so brave, was terrified at the thought of crossing the sea, of boarding a ship, of taking his place in a boat, to the extent that people sometimes laughed at this huge warrior who always tried to keep his feet dry and grew worried at the smallest brook.

While Elzéar was saying his first words and learning his prayers, bands of Turkmens on small, lively horses emerged from the darkness of my nights, swarms of turbaned riders harassing the long line of Crusaders, jabbing like flies at that huge, slow body of Christians on their way to the tomb of Christ, then vanishing amid the stones. Only Gauvin, Amaury de Joux's incredible mount—whose white coat turned red during battles and who was more like a wild beast than a horse—sometimes managed to catch up with one of these phantom riders, and Amaury would bring back a corpse, thus proving to his companions that their attackers were nothing but men.

Through my father's eyes, I saw the emperor reach Cilicia and hesitate to cross the river Cydnos, whose limpid but icy waters had already almost carried away Alexander some centuries earlier, I saw him advance cautiously and disappear suddenly into that little river, as if his nightmare had caught up with him, disappear with horse and armor, after struggling, sword in hand, against the icy blue of the waters, disappear before the eyes of all his men, who were astonished to see him thus drown in a river so calm and so shallow.

I saw the rout of the army of the Holy Roman Empire after their leader was swallowed by the Cydnos, I saw those great lords scatter in all directions in their dismay, returning home with their men to their wives and their lands, refusing, after the only man whose footsteps had ever made the great Saladin tremble had drowned so incredibly, to follow his water-swollen corpse—a corpse that his third son, Frederick of Swabia, soaked in vinegar in order to preserve it and lead it where his adversaries were waiting for it, in Jerusalem.

According to those who returned, a dead warrior, however prestigious, could neither retake a city nor win back Christ's tomb from the Saracens. Perhaps even the deceased emperor, seeing his troops disintegrate and the finest of armies reduced to a handful of madmen, ceased to believe it, since his corpse, despite the vinegar, ended up giving off such as stench that it was necessary to abandon his decomposing body on the journey and leave it in the church of St. Peter in Antioch— although his son retrieved a few bones, which he planned to bury on Mount Golgotha.

Imagine, you who are listening to me in the shadows, imagine an army of more than a hundred thousand men, the most imposing army ever raised, an army whose songs had been echoing in the ears of the great Saladin for months, an army swarming with men driven by faith and hatred, imagine this army brought to a halt by a measly little river, dissolved in one meter of water, reduced by the sudden death of a man who had been so terrified of water since the beginning of the journey that he had not drunk a single drop of it for months and grew anxious at the thought of having to wash himself.

And my father continued to walk in Elzéar's hands, and, in those holes he had pierced in them though his madness, I saw him advance along the shores of the Mediterranean, in the company of a few hundred stubborn men who, after carrying their drowned emperor's corpse for many leagues, after living with its stench, and after finally laying down their rotting burden in Antioch, had decided to walk in high summer, beneath that notorious, deadly sun my father dreaded so much, as far as Acre, clinging to their dreams of victory, even if it meant dying along the way, as so many of their brothers had already died. They even joked about it, telling each other that it would be easy to retrace their steps when they could no longer go on, because so many corpses lay strewn in their wake.

My brother Guillaume was among the bodies abandoned on the journey. He had succumbed to one of the nameless fevers only found in those lands choked with silt, and my father had had to cover his dead child with stones and tears, while Thierry II, who now regarded him as the only friend he had ever had, blessed the makeshift grave from which my father had no wish to tear himself. On the horizon, the figures of their companions were already blurring in the furnace-like heat, but my father refused to obey Thierry and rise to his feet. He blamed himself for dragging his sons all this way for a sin that he alone had committed, including them in his death, for fear no doubt of experiencing that death alone and far from home, for fear they would not hear his last words and that nobody would be there to carve his name on his tombstone. And now it was he who had heard his child's last fever-laden sigh and clumsily carved on a stone with the point of his knife the name he had given him at birth. This was something he had never envisaged. He screamed his great sin to the desert. How could he have believed so firmly that he was the center of the world? How could he not have realized earlier that he was not the only one whose life would be put in danger by this terrible journey?

Thierry had comforted his friend for a long time before the latter calmed down and agreed to set off again, to catch up with those of his children who, unsteady on their feet as they might be, were at least still standing.

Barbarossa's son led the march. He had wrapped his father's bones in a sack that he never let out of his sight, and each of the Crusaders had lost a little of his blood on the journey, to the extent that fathers and sons, dead and alive, walked together now, and every day there were more and more ghosts—much to the consternation of the Saracens, who no longer dared attack a caravan that numbered so many specters. I myself could no longer distinguish those hearts that had stopped beating from those that still beat faintly, or make out who was carrying whom, the sons or the fathers, the living or the dead. All these walking corpses stooped beneath their crosses, the blood red of which was turning ocher, for the colors themselves were fading, eaten away by the same deadly sun. And in the middle of these dead men stubbornly hanging on and these living men on their last legs, Thierry II, thinner than ever, almost desiccated beneath his grey miter, still gave voice to his unshakable faith, and, when he was not praying, continued to elaborate out loud the engine of iron and wood he was convinced would open the gates of Jerusalem to them.

The horses had been drained of their blood and eaten on the way. Only Gauvin had been spared. Amaury de Joux had preferred to chase it away in order to shield it from the fate of its brothers, and not a day went by without his companions seeing that extraordinary white horse in the distance, raising clouds of sand beneath its hooves. Overwhelmed with fatigue, the Crusaders could not make up their minds if it was a mirage, a ghost, or if the powerful animal was watching over its master from a distance.

As they approached the end of their journey, Frederick of Swabia was finding the going increasingly difficult. His father's white bones weighed ever more heavily on him, as if they had continued to take in water, as if it were no longer just relics that he bore on his back, but the whole of the Cydnos, that tiny river laden now with the mad dream it had devoured, the dream of the greatest army ever raised, and Frederick of Swabia, thinking that he was transporting the emperor's remains, was in fact dragging his father's dream, like a huge chimera curled up in a soft leather bag. In the end, the son was obliged to abandon his father's remains for a second time and to lay down his burden in Tyre, where Frederick Barbarossa's bones, apart from his skull, were buried, while his soldiers, living and dead, looked on wearily.

Now you see why I so dreaded sleep! My four hours of sleep a day would take me to the desert and I would return from it exhausted, barely capable of praying to support my father and my brothers on the terrible path I had driven them to take.

Then, waking bathed in sweat, I would gently free myself from the arms of the child who was forcing me to see my family's ordeal as if a long chain of sorrows bound us one to the other merely because we shared the same blood. As if, like water, that blood always tended to come together in a single drop. I would light a candle to chase away the eastern sun whose glare had burned my eyes, and, once the dazzle had faded, I would look at my child sleeping with his mouth open, his little body abandoned in my tomb. His long lashes sometimes fluttered . . .

My gaze had touched him, very lightly.

At the age of almost three, Elzéar was able, by pushing my chair as close as possible to the wall, to hoist himself up to the bars over my window and slide through to the ground on the other side. He was freer than I had ever been, even though he slept in my cell. I did not constrain him to that tiny space but let him leap about outside as he wished. I even helped him when he escaped like that, concealing the anguish that increasingly took hold of me whenever we parted. For, as Elzéar gained in agility, it became more difficult for him to worm his way between the bars in order to run to the stables and watch the men working there. I would follow him with my eyes for as long as possible, then try to imagine his games, putting together what I could on the basis of what everybody told me about them. Elzéar would also try to tell me of his discoveries, in his own incoherent way, but his world was one of fragments and he still lacked the words as well as the ability to organize his memories in time and space.

His pierced hands gave me access only to my father's eyes—curiously, anything just beyond the great maple was more distant to me than Syria, Hell, or Heaven—and my nights were always filled with his sufferings, which Elzéar's daily caresses condemned me to share.

I was experiencing his ordeal from within—I was his feet, his eyes, his flesh. I was attached to my father like the mistletoe to the tree. I espoused his thoughts as clearly as on the evening of my abortive wedding.

*

In Tyre, despite their extreme fatigue, my father and his companions in misfortune had been unable to find sleep, so troubled were their nights by the demands of the ghosts. I sensed that they would not rest until they, too, died, or until they led these specters where they were urging them to be led. They had only a few leagues left to travel in order to join the troops who had been besieging Acre for several months. But they were like armed corpses, worn down by hunger, pain, and sun, and I did not see how they could take even one more step. Yet the dead would not let go of them, the dead and their unrealized dreams of glory harassed them ceaselessly, screaming in their skulls like seabirds high in the sky, to such an extent that the gulls flying over the city of Tyre seemed to be echoing their cries. An army was howling inside the heads of those who were not yet dead—they could not be dead, because their broken bodies still hurt so much, but, hearing the cries of the dead they had abandoned on the way, they knew that they were already close to the banks of the Styx. This frontier was untenable, they had to find a way to satisfy these specters, of whom they were nothing but the receptacles, to help them pay the price of their passage, to lead them into the battle that would grant them forgiveness and open the gates of Heaven to them. The survivors of the army of the Holy Roman Empire therefore resolved to obey those stubborn dead who said they had carried them this far—even though it was unclear who had carried whom—and submitted to the mad will of that battalion of shades whose dead voices refused to be silent, voices that I myself heard in my cell, as distinctly as you hear my whispers today.

Only a few of them, including Amey, Amaury de Joux—still mourning his Gauvin—Thierry, and my father, were able to procure new mounts to replace the animals whose blood they had had to drink and whose flesh they had had to eat on the journey, but all of them, whether on foot or on horseback, left the shadow of the city to pursue their Crusade.

Carrying their tattered banners and displaying their blood-stained crosses on their bodies, the survivors of the greatest army in the world arrived within sight of Acre, the walls of which plunged sheer into the sea.

From the promontory where my father stood, I could see the whole of that city of stone, withdrawn behind its walls, as if driven back toward the waves, and that other city that faced it, a vast, ramshackle city of canvas, built by the Crusaders, spread over the whole chain of hills surrounding the plain where Acre was situated. And beyond those hills, my father and his companions tried to detect the fires of Saladin's encampments, which they imagined on another, even wider concentric semicircle.

They had at last reached the first destination that they had fixed for themselves when they left their cottages and castles and churches. They had reached this place where all the forces of Christendom had arranged to meet, this city they would have to retake before launching themselves on Jerusalem.

Silently, they sat down for a moment on the stones, they sat down side by side, the living and the dead, they stopped at the edge of the picture to await their leader—for Frederick of Swabia, dragging with him in his soft leather pouch the last relic of his father, that skull heavy with the grandest of dreams and a host of shades, was advancing even less quickly than they were, although they had thought of themselves as motionless.

They sat down and contemplated the battle raging in the plain. A nameless pestilence rose from an abyss filled with sun and pain. They saw the Crusaders crushed like ants beneath the walls of Acre, their corpses heaped up to fill the ditches and make it easier to raise the siege ladders, while Saladin's horsemen took advantage to attack their deserted city of canvas from the rear and put it to the torch. They could make out a huge tower above the sea, a tower as large as an arch, which the Christians had brought with them on a ship, and which was now attacking the city. They watched as this improbable construction, full to bursting with men-at-arms, changed into an incandescent torch and was swallowed by the waters. They watched, powerless, as their side was defeated by earth and sea, all the while waiting for the skull of the emperor at whose urging they had come to this place.

Imagine, you who are listening to me, imagine the disappointment of the Franks when they returned to their ruined camp, still reeling from their double defeat, and saw that wretched troop of dying men shuffling toward them, their huge, empty eyes seeming to devour their emaciated faces. Imagine the bitterness felt by those who for months had been expecting the imminent arrival of this army of the Holy Roman Empire, which had been described to them as the finest and most orderly in the world. Imagine their astonishment when they realized that the reinforcements they had so long awaited had been reduced to this handful of starving beggars, these few emaciated puppets, manipulated by cantankerous ghosts who had come to them to demand their due.

Every army had its jargon, its quarters, its provisions, its artisans, and its stalls. Surrounded by hostile eyes, Frederick of Swabia was looking for a place to stop in the chaos of tents. Shortages were beginning to proliferate, and nobody was thrilled at the thought of welcoming these tramps laden with nothing but their own folly, these remnants of a disaster dragging with them a skull in a leather pouch. They were suspected of bringing bad luck, and some avoided touching even their shadows for fear of being contaminated by misfortune. As if encysted in my father's mind, I heard through his ears the mockery that surrounded these newcomers, the malevolent whispers accusing them of bearing the stench of death. Each in his own patois, the soldiers cursed them as they passed, asserting that it would have been better for Christendom if they had all drowned in that river that had carried away their leader.

They were assigned a dusty patch of ground somewhat to one side, not far from the corner reserved for lepers.

As insensitive to fatigue as to despair, Thierry II immediately unpacked his kit, and my father, who was helping him, was surprised to find in it nothing but heavy treatises on geometry and architecture, containing the principles behind engines of war, and rolls of parchment covered in notes and drawings. In Antioch, the archbishop had exchanged his precious illuminated Bible for the plans of an ingenious system for moving wheels that made it possible to reduce the number of men necessary to prepare the most imposing war machines. But around this extraordinary diagram, doubtless stolen from some Saracen engineer, all the notes were in Arabic, and that elegant gibberish reduced the archbishop to hysteria. As soon as he was settled, he crisscrossed the camp, accompanied by my father, in search of a man sufficiently knowledgeable to decipher these notes, as well as craftsmen capable of realizing the machine that had been haunting him since the beginning of the journey, and of which this plan seemed to resolve one of the thorniest problems, that of weight. Eventually, just a few days after his arrival, he was presented with a remarkable man who, having worked for a time at the court of Saladin, immediately recognized in the diagram the genius of Murda al-Tarsûsî, one of the most brilliant Muslim engineers of his time. From that point onward, the project benefited from the support of the whole of Christendom, and Thierry II was supplied with as much money and as many carpenters as he wanted. It was essential that the incredible trebuchet he had been inventing throughout the journey, whenever he was not praying, be built as quickly as possible, so that their camp might benefit from a body of knowledge stolen from the enemy.

One week after his pitiful arrival, Frederick of Swabia, still goaded by specters, decided to launch a surprise attack on the outposts of Saladin's army, in order to steal enough to feed that wretched, skeletal troop and prove his valor to all those terrified by his misfortune. But that day, the only thing that surprised the Muslim warriors was the thinness of their attackers, whose bones came and shattered on their sabers like insects throwing themselves into the flames. My father knew how weary his companions were: he himself was fighting now only for his sons, whom he had been stupid enough to drag with him. Death had cut down such a large number of those desperate men during that mad venture that for a time it seemed as though it had had its fill. The ghosts, clustered about the survivors, at last ceased their chatter, and they were all able to return to their tents and sleep as much as they wanted. Some achieved a sleep so deep that they never awoke again.

The building of Thierry II's monstrous trebuchet continued while winter flooded the plain of Acre, transforming it into a vile swamp where the corpses rotted. The foul breath of death contaminated the living, and diseases struck the two cities, that of stone and that of canvas, indiscriminately. A tiny wooden church had been built by an English priest right in the middle of this muddy charnel house and, like Charon crossing the Styx, his brown figure could be seen, as soon as dawn broke, crossing the mist-shrouded marsh, piling the dead onto a handcart, and giving them a makeshift burial near his rickety chapel.

One morning, my father noticed that an animal had been harnessed to that terrible cart. Head bowed, a skeletal horse with a mud-stained coat was slowly dragging the dead into the plain. So someone had finally offered that poor Charon a nag to help him in his superhuman enterprise! The gift surprised my father all the more since horses were becoming rare in the encampments. As the boats, haunted by the bad weather, were no longer bringing in supplies to anyone, there was as much hunger in one camp as in the other. Those Crusaders who still possessed provisions hid them underground, or spent a fortune on a horse's innards, and my father, like other lords, was sometimes reduced to grazing the wild grass that still grew between the stones and chewing roots.

The sharp bitter taste of the earthy plants my father masticated to assuage his hunger stuck to my palate, and I had all the trouble in the world to remove it from my mouth when, at last extricating myself from sleep, I tore myself from his poor weakened carcass and rejoined my own body in its cell.

Every night, I plunged back into Hell, living what my father was living, seeing what he saw, eating what he ate. My son's hands spared me none of his sufferings, and this strange communion of pain was nothing like that I had hoped to live in Christ.

During that siege of Acre, famine and disease proved far deadlier than the battles, and I shuddered with horror the day the man whose blood, name, and eyes I shared had, within a period of a few hours, to close the eyes of his second son, Jean, and those of Frederick of Swabia, both carried away by the same disease. I saw his thin fingers come to rest on their moist eyelids with the same paternal tenderness. Nothing drove him now but that tenderness, that gentle feeling of which he had never been aware before this final rout. Without any sense of rebellion, without any pride or any strength, completely deprived of what he had long thought essential to a man of his caliber, my father realized that tenderness would be his last feeling, that it alone had been able to withstand this horrible war that was called holy, that it alone was still keeping him alive, even though he had spent most of his life either ignoring it or fighting it.

He took charge of the soft leather pouch that still contained the relic of an emperor whose name nobody any longer wished to utter, and, with the help of his few remaining companions, transported the two corpses to the Englishman's church, stuck halfway to Hell. There, for the last time, Thierry II and that strange Charon blessed Jean, Frederick of Swabia, and the Emperor's skull—which was now empty of all hope and as light as a nutshell, as if depopulated by this ultimate defeat—and then buried them in the clay.

Then the priest's nag, that pitiful horse with the muddy coat, which was holding itself at a distance from the handful of Crusaders assembled there, its eyes dull, its spine low, as if weighed down by the folly of men and exhausted by the corpse-laden carts it had had to pull up out of the mud, suddenly gave a long sigh such as only beasts are capable of.

No, truly, men were not a pretty sight! Better they all die, the horse seemed to be saying.

"Where did you get that jade?" my father asked the priest.

"It came to me, but I have almost nothing to offer it as a reward for the help it has given me. Like a stray dog, it finds its food in the marshes, grazing on what it can find among the decomposing bodies. It eats the grass of the dead. I am not certain it will long survive such a diet. It's a fine animal, and appears to understand our sufferings and to both judge us and pity us."

At this point, Amaury went up to the poor beast, which was dozing and not looking at him, and stroked its neck. A flame suddenly appeared in the horse's big, glassy eyes—a fleeting gleam thanks to which Amaury recognized Gauvin, that miraculous stallion that now, having been reduced to a mere shadow of itself, took interest in nothing but the dead. Weeping, Amaury de Joux embraced Gauvin like a brother, and the horse rubbed its great, sad head against its master's shoulder. Amaury threw himself onto its back, and in the flash of an eye transformed the jade into a charger, revived it, awakened it, set in on fire. The animal's muscles quivered beneath its soiled coat, and Amaury regained that nobility he only had on horseback, while Gauvin stamped as it had in its glory days. It was strange, such thinness combined with all that old power, that strength recovered in the space of an instant. Perhaps it was Amaury's corpse the magnificent stallion had been desperately searching for in that charnel house, in order to carry him to the other shore, to transport him into the afterlife. The man had resumed his place on the beast's back, in a perfect harmony that glorified them both, and, as if their spines had been stiffened by the memory of what they had once been, the formidable couple set off at top speed, straight across the enemy lines. Realizing where Gauvin was taking him at this mad pace, Amaury drew his sword, turned toward those of his comrades who were still alive, and bade them one last farewell. Then horse and man threw themselves together into death.

The few bloodless survivors who witnessed this last stand of a centaur, these men whose clay was barely alive—to the extent that the dead, wearied perhaps by the fact that they could no longer rouse them as they wished, had finally left them alone—waited several weeks before deciding that the pair could be declared lost forever.

It was then that Amey de Montfaucon, Lothaire's brother, immediately regained his vigor and decided to return home to announce her widowhood to the pretty Berthe, the woman he had loved madly before she had married Amaury de Joux. He managed to embark on a ship leaving for Italy. To Amey's care my father entrusted Benjamin, his youngest son, the only one remaining to him on this side of the world, and he wept as he watched him sail away from the shore, he wept without even finding the strength to raise his arm and wave him farewell. Then, once the child had left, he lay down on the earth of that land called holy, on that earth gorged with Muslim, Christian, Jewish, and Philistine blood, which was not only the cradle of a violent humanity, but the sacrificial stone where the sons of a single God killed each other like dogs in His name, yes, not only the beginning, but the final end, the tomb of humankind. He lay on his back on the icy ground beneath a night sky as full of holes as a moth-eaten canopy and thought about me, confined between my walls, and about Elzéar and Phébus, who by now were walking, and about Douce's long scented hair, and about the warm bodies of young girls, fragile shells he had once held in his hands, and I discovered how much he regretted having tried to break the finest of them all by deflowering her in the bracken. He thought of his sin, walled up within him as I was in my cell, and he decided to let it out, to reveal it to that man of God who had become his friend, for he alone might perhaps listen to him with benevolence.

In the morning, he went straight to the construction site where the archbishop had pitched his tent. The battalion of carpenters and blacksmiths working there to build the engines of war imagined by Thierry II had not yet begun their day's labor. At first light, the place was deserted, and, like all Crusaders, my father felt a surge of emotion as he approached the most incredible of all these engines, that formidable trebuchet beside which all other such machines were relegated to the ranks of mere children's games. Acre would surrender at the mere sight of the monster, there was no doubt about it.

"Have you come to admire my masterpiece?" asked the archbishop, delighted to see how astonished his vassal was at the sight of that huge, dark, almost unreal mass whose giant arm rose toward the sky.

"No, I've come to speak to a friend."

Thierry invited him into his tent and bade him sit.

"I am Elzéar's father," my father confessed, broken not by his successive losses or by hunger, but by that sin which, although his, had somehow gone beyond him and, in his sick mind, was responsible for the failure of this whole lamentable expedition.

As the archbishop said nothing, he continued, "I forced

Esclarmonde on the morning of her entombment, and pierced our son's palms with a sledgehammer and a big nail on the day of his birth. She did not lie to you and your entourage, she simply answered the questions you asked and not those you did not ask. Do not judge her silence, she is upright and will not lie if she is asked one day who Elzéar father is and how he got his stigmata."

Without a word, Thierry simply took his friend's pierced hand affectionately in his own—gloveless for months and scored by the chisel, the drill, and all those tools he had learned to handle on his construction site—and the two men sat thus in silence, clinging to one another like two shipwreck survivors.

The very day of this confession, my father caught his friend dispatching a mute cleric to the earldom of Burgundy with a sealed message for both Esclarmonde the anchoress and the man Thierry foresaw would soon be his successor as Archbishop of Besançon, and through my father's eyes I saw the face of that cleric more than a year before he appeared before my window and delivered to me the posthumous order of Archbishop Thierry II. I did not then know the contents of that order, but, during all the time that long journey lasted, I correctly thought of it as fate on the march, an order sent out on the roads with the intention of protecting the chapter of Saint-Jean from the weakness its leader had shown on the day when, believing for a moment in the beauty of the world, the strength of the weak, and the divine glow of a bastard, he had blessed that living lie: my son.

By early April, the arrival of the kings of France and England beneath the walls of Acre was imminent. They would soon be landing on the coast with their formidable armies, but Thierry II did not want to leave them the honors of a victory that his engine would give them, so, without waiting for them, his giant trebuchet was pushed out onto the dried-up plain on a spring day almost nauseatingly heavy with scents.

The skeletal archbishop with the long, pale face—a narrow mask of dry wood pierced with coal-black eyes and crowned with a newly-dusted miter glittering with gilt and precious stones, huge hands again gloved in white, a broad chasuble concealing the absence of flesh, seated on a horse that was just skin and bone and gesticulating with the crozier in his hand like some puppet animated by a hysterical puppet master— rode forward only a few paces ahead of his formidable engine.

Excited at the thought of soon seeing his invention spit out the cannonballs specially cut for it out of the thickest rocks of Etna, this crowned bag of bones did not notice the motionless brown child, armed with a sling and five small pointed stones, who was watching him—and his engine—from the hole where he had lodged himself. My father suddenly saw this boy emerge from his hiding place and stand firm, a tiny figure in the path of that Goliath of wood and iron. This time, David did not aim at the giant. He calmly stared at Thierry II and fired a stone that hit the archbishop in the middle of his forehead.

Thierry collapsed, victim of a simple sling identical to the one with which—or so he had told my father—he had so often played as a child before it was confiscated from him. In his fall, he seemed to come apart, to be broken up into those elements that even a few moments earlier had already seemed to have so much difficulty holding together—miter, crook, chasuble, wooden face, glittering eyes, gloved bones—and all these pieces fell in a heap one on top of the other, as if the poor puppet had been completely fleshless, and this final shock had cut the threads of the outfit that had still managed somehow to contain it.

When my father saw his friend collapse to the ground—and realized that the trebuchet was following its creator too closely to avoid the little bag of bones and cloth to which the throwing of a stone had reduced him—it struck him that it was only fair that Thierry should die thus, brought down by a child like the little boy he had been, armed with a simple sling like the one he had once made for himself.

Yes, it was only fair, he told himself later, that he should fall thus beneath the wheels of his own masterpiece and that he should not witness the fabulous trebuchet sink into the plain of Acre—doubtless the weight of the engine would remain an insoluble problem.

Only my father was left now.

My old nurse with her dried-up breasts became more insistent when my child reached the age of three.

She had remained on her patch of land all winter and had not appeared at the castle. Her stride had diminished to an infinite degree. She walked now with the help of a stick, which one of her sons had carefully cut and polished for her in the evening before the main fire of their dwelling.

She attended the service in my chapel, sitting right at the back on a bench that Douce had installed there for her, then advanced alone through that mist in which the world had been enveloped since her pupils had become veiled with a milky cloud. Keeping close to the wall of Sainte-Agnès, she came and sat down outside my cell. We waited for a while, face to face, until her hoarse breathing settled and she could at last speak. I hung on the slightest flutter of her eyelashes.

"Esclarmonde," she said in a solemn tone, "you must hear me and not put off your decision any longer. According to Ivette, it's getting harder and harder for your son to leave your tomb. If you wait any longer before weaning Elzéar from your presence, you will condemn him to be walled up, and that wouldn't be his choice, but yours. As he grows, he would hate you for imprisoning him in that cell."

"I have not yet known solitude, since Elzéar lived in me after my entombment. I have never felt less alone than I have since his birth. I know perfectly well that this separation must come, that all ladies know it when their sons leave them to live in

another house as pages. In my class, the mother is always separated from her child. I envy you villeins and serfs for keeping
them with you longer, for not having to extricate them a second time from your bodies."

"It's usually death that cuts that invisible tie. I've lost so
many of my children that all their little graves with the wooden
crosses above them are like a forest."

"You still live with two of your grown children, you sleep
beside them. You will no doubt die amid the uproar of your family, hearing your son's children whining around your deathbed.
You will never know the silence of a fire without a child."

"Don't envy us too much, Esclarmonde. It's our poverty
that forces us to remain so close together. And if I live too long,
I'll be a burden for my family, another mouth to feed, without
the strength to tell stories in the evening, or to advise everyone,
or to do her share. Already I can no longer bend to gather my
dandelions. These simple acts are gradually becoming impossible for me, and that's taking me farther and farther from my
family. I'm terrified at the thought of becoming just a weak
body, lying in a corner of the room, unable to do anything but
moan with pain and anguish, a body everyone would like to
silence at night when they lie down before the fire and try to
sleep, a creature condemned to be a nuisance to the living,
clinging to life without anyone understanding why, a useless
old woman who's gone back to being a child to be suckled at
the breast."

"You'll never be a burden to your children, they respect
you. The position you occupy among them today is one of wisdom and authority, but even if those things go, you will always
have their love."

"My daughter, you have no idea what you're talking about.
I know the weight of things, the strength of love, the torture of
slow death. Love remains a memory, and we eat on the graves
of the dead to keep them quiet, but dying is an ordeal for those

who are forced to witness it, especially where love is involved. To become a burden to those I've carried in my flesh, in my arms, in my heart, would be the worst of ends. Yes, better to leave first, better not to last so long."

"Do you know how old you are?"

"No, but it was I who ripped your father from his mother's belly. The child had such a pointed skull, I had to knead it for days on end like a big lump of butter. I'm the oldest servant at the Whispers, the one who knows the children of its children. There's no word in our language to describe me. They call men grandfathers, so I could be called a grandmother. I sometimes think I'm the oldest woman in the world. It's been a long time since I last had anyone ahead of me. They've all gone, all the people I could talk to about the old days. My world is dead."

"You have lived a long time!"

"It's because I'm a hard worker, and my children came easily, like water. And besides, death has withdrawn from this fiefdom since you started praying for us. For almost four years now, he's forgotten all of us, including me."

"He must be doubly busy elsewhere."

"Tell him not to linger all the same. I'm very weary."

A flock of starlings came to rest in the maple, and for a moment the tree was alive with song. Then, all together, as if driven by a common whim, the birds rose again, chirping, and described their mad arabesques in the sky. Fleeting signs traced in the air, which neither of us could any longer see, but which we had observed so often, wondering if one of the birds imposed a rhythm on all the others or if they merely obeyed in unison the silent orders of the wind.

"Don't keep the child with you, Esclarmonde! Give him back to the world!"

"He'll think I'm abandoning him."

"He should be kept outside, well away from your cell, until the day it's impossible for him to return. I'll keep him with me for as long as it takes. When I'm quite certain he'll never again be able to pass through these bars, I'll take him back to the castle."

"Then we will live each on different sides of the world. This frontier of stone and iron has never seemed to me an obstacle, I crossed it every day through Elzéar's eyes, I lived his first steps in the grass, I accompanied him on the carpets of the ladies' chamber, I enjoyed his first times. In my cell, I rediscovered a tenderness that had been but a luminous memory, a tenderness I'll again have to do without, just like when my mother died. Let me wait until the last moment. He's still suckling at my breast."

"Prepare yourself, my girl, I'll come soon to take him. It's high time, believe me."

After she left, I thought about the Virgin, and it struck me that there was something miraculous in the figure of the mother with her child and in the love that unites them, and that God himself had been sufficiently moved by it to want to savor this feeling that He had not created, this force born outside of Him and of which He knew nothing. It struck me that God the Father had established that love as a model, that love from which He was absent. The Father had driven his son to sacrifice, and although the Mother had not argued with the divine plan, she had suffered it infinitely in her flesh, in her soul.

The Virgin was crucified under Pontius Pilate, she suffered her passion.

Yes, the Virgin too was on the Cross.

I did not sleep for several weeks, in order to remain as close as possible to my child and not have to join my father. I did not feel capable of adding his despair to mine. One evening I finally abandoned myself to sleep, and my dreams immediately caught up with me and dragged me to the other side of the world.

The hour was approaching.

I had left my father at the end of spring, when the two kings, Richard and Philippe Auguste, had just come together before Acre and it was rumored that the city, its strength exhausted, would soon be laying down its arms. And now I found him alone, far from the sea, lost on the roads, I found him aged, half-mad, advancing bareheaded beneath a leaden sun. He was talking to himself, accusing himself of being the man who had caused the disaster, the one who, by flaying his own flesh, had brought down all the stars in the sky, one by one. And he said he had seen those stars throbbing for a time in the dust, slowly dying like fish out of water before expiring completely. Motionless, he had witnessed the slaughter of the stars. He had seen the eyes of the children of Acre tarnished with the blood of their mothers, and the sky was now nothing but one vast hole.

There was no saliva left in his mouth and yet he spoke, moving that piece of dry flesh that served him as a tongue, endlessly passing the back of his hand over his mouth to try to prize his lips apart, to wipe away the sticky white deposit that had formed on them and to free his inarticulate speech from those shreds of burned skin that obstructed it. Occasionally, he would look up at the skies as if cursing the sun.

Now I was again trapped inside him, in a body so thin and dry that it seemed ready to burst into flame or dissolve into ash beneath the white-hot sky. *Remember that thou art dust.* My father spoke in the burning heat of noon and his voice, his expression, his clothes were so wretched that none of the villagers he met dreamed of calling him an infidel. Nobody tried to stop him, but many gave him food and drink without his even needing to ask—which he would have been quite incapable of doing, so far had he abandoned himself on this last journey. They fed this Christian with his confused mind, who could no longer express his hunger or his pain even though he spoke ceaselessly in his mysterious jargon. He had escaped from the epicenter of the war and was wandering in a place where men still had human faces. But the old man carried his nightmare in his eyes, and the fellahs sensed that he no longer had much left on his horizon, that he was approaching his end. So they stood aside to let the old Frank pass and prayed to Allah to grant peace to this poor madman gibbering in the blinding dust of words that no one could grasp—not even I, even though I was lodged in his mind—and these words were so like the groans of the damned that those who heard them were overcome with horror.

I walked in the footsteps of this man who was crumbling into words, I walked without understanding either his slow sentences or where he was leading us with his shuffling gait. I walked barefoot on the burning sands, and the stones gashed our calloused skin down to the bone.

God wanted me close to my father in his death agony, and refusing to sleep would make no difference.

Nevertheless I resisted and escaped the dream, but in my tomb the sun was still there when I awoke, its light concealed my child from me, and not even all the water I then drank could quench that thirst that was not mine even though it burned my throat. I opened my shutter, hoping to dispel the dust and the blazing light of the desert. But the white glare swallowed everything—the great maple, the dawn, the court-yard—and it took me time to recover from that blindness. The two visions were superimposed, and in the frame of my window, all barred with metal and deadly sun, I at last made out the figure of my old nurse advancing painfully toward me, sup-ported by one of her sons. Through my father's groans, I rec-ognized the unsteady stride of the woman who was coming to take Elzéar from me.

For the first time, I was both here and elsewhere, my eyes were still also my father's eyes, the dream blurred my sight, it had poured into my life even beyond waking, it was insistent, clinging to my pupils, forcing me to submit, to close my eyes again in order to eliminate at least one of the two images. Death was entering my body—that death that was not mine, but my father's—and I could not turn away from it, I heard its cold little voice singing us a lullaby, I felt it rise along my father's legs as if he were sinking into icy water, and, in his last moments, as the sun devoured our eyes, the old woman, sway-ing there on the other side of the world, demanded to take my child from me forever.

Yes, it was time.

If Elzéar left, perhaps I might be spared living my father's death agony to the bitter end, perhaps he would die without a witness!

In his madness, he approached a hole between the stones, a narrow rift into which he had decided to worm his way to escape the violence of the sun.

At that moment Elzéar awoke, as if startled by my father's attempt to sink into that burning breach. I took my child in my arms and was unable to stop his pierced little hands from playing a moment longer over my eyes, driving other images into my skull, like splinters.

At last, my son saw the old woman outside, gently shaking the bridle of an old horse, urging him to join her, and my child, still damp from sleep, hugged me to him, while I felt my father's weather-beaten skin rub against the rock as he forced himself into that narrow basin in the earth, and my child, wanting to join the old horse, escaped from me and stuck his temples between the bars to get out. I gritted my teeth in order not to scream, I swallowed my cry as I had on the morning of his birth.

Elzéar was outside on the back of the old horse—oh, the weight of his body in my arms!—and my father was huddling in a tiny cave as white as milk.

My son waved his small pierced hands one last time in my direction, delighted that he was about to go on an excursion far from me, far from the mother who had borne him thus far—oh, the weight of his body in me—and my father curled up in that chalk bosom. His right hand played for a while with the clear sand, letting it trickle slowly between his fingers.

My child disappeared behind the great maple.

My father grew silent, his arm falling back into the dust the color of milk.

And I sank into a dreamless sleep, as if dying.

Elzéar would return to the Whispers, I just had to wait. A few moons, two or three seasons, perhaps a whole year. He would return, he would return to the Whispers. But never again would I be the arms in which he huddled as if within himself. He would return, but that second cord that is a mother's caress would be broken and never again would we savor that sublime closeness of mother and child. He would return, he would return . . .

Oh, my love! I could no longer remember living a single day without you. I could no longer remember the young girl I had been, or how she had occupied her time before you came and devoured it.

My little ogre had left me, laughing, on his old horse. Would he even remember his mother when he was brought back to the Whispers?

After his departure, I no longer had the strength to welcome the pilgrims or even to pray for them. The universe had been torn apart and my belly was like stone, empty and cold.

Summer held sway on the other side of the bars, but it made no difference to me. Sorrow is a season unto itself.

I stopped eating, although this time there was nothing religious about my fast. Not being carried along by my faith, I soon grew very weak, and those close to me tried to find a way to shield me from a death that was beginning to be a colorless presence behind my eyes. Ivette spread the rumor that whoever looked into my eyes could now see a shadow struggling within them. According to her, Death was being held captive in those pale blue circles. Had I imprisoned him in my eyes by watching him at work so much through my father's eyes? The fact remains that he had not put in another appearance in the houses of the fiefdom and the boldest of the young people, thinking themselves safe within the sphere of my prayer, were beginning to mock him and to abandon all caution.

The Grim Reaper was waiting in the shadows, biding his time.

One midsummer noon, Bérengère chased away her entourage of suitors and advanced alone toward me in the sun.

The ends of her green skirt undulated so harmoniously around her curves, it was as if the Loue itself—that river veiled in places by long, languid strands of seaweed breaking the surface at the whim of the current—was coming majestically to meet me. My mind was so blurred by hunger that I actually thought Bérengère with her flowing movements was gradually turning into a river. Were not her pupils and her long, fair hair heavy with shades of green? She must have been the victim of some spell to draw all the men in the region behind her, I thought, trying to see my hazy reflection on her surface, as if on the surface of a wave.

"Why don't you come back to the world?" she asked me in her deep, husky voice. "It's easy enough to knock down this awful wall with a sledgehammer and free you from the stones."

"And how do you hope to free me from my promise?"

"I don't understand what you mean! You're twenty at the most, and you have a life waiting for you out here, but you just stay there in your tomb! What are you afraid of? The world outside? Your father's return? Poor Lothaire? The desire that boy sublimates into songs?"

"My father will not return. I saw him dying in my son's

hands, although I've said nothing yet to Douce. Guillaume and Jean are dead too. Only Benjamin is on his way back here in the company of Amey de Montfaucon. As for Lothaire, it is true that I've never feared him as much as I fear him now. But neither his passion nor his poems would keep me locked up here . . . There remains the world. I've learned in my cell how vast and sublime it is. I've learned that however far you go you will never get to the end. Travelers have allowed me to see the fabulous landscapes they crossed by merely moving their feet forward. What a wonder for a walled-up woman to imagine herself crisscrossing such a vast universe! What intoxication it must be to walk so simply without anything to stop the eye, and to feel the earth beating beneath one's heels, and to breathe in deeply the breath of the world!"

"Martin can get you out of here. He's not the kind of man to let the walls of a chapel stop him. I have the guards eating out of my hand, I'll see to them while he smashes through the stones."

"And what then? The Church doesn't let Her anchoresses escape so easily. And just to imagine myself fleeing Her hand, alone and defenseless on the roads with Elzéar, makes my head spin."

"Then ask the chapter of Saint-Jean to free you from your vow. I'm quite happy to serve as your envoy."

"Only the Pope could reopen my sepulcher and return me to the life I left."

"Then write to the Pope, you can use a pen, you aren't like the rest of us who have to entrust our words to the wind! I'll go all the way to Rome and take him your letter."

"You would have so few opportunities to reach him."

"I'm a lot stronger than I seem."

"And what explanation would I give for my request? That the holy woman who gave birth to a child in her tomb is unable to live far from him? That God is no longer enough for me?

That's not the way to protect Elzéar. If I leave my hole I renounce any claim to holiness, and in doing so I condemn my son, whose mysterious birth will soon set tongues wagging. I have to keep my place, the better to protect him."

"Then feed yourself and don't let yourself be carried away by sorrow! Elzéar is happy in Ivette's family, he's grown very fond of the old horse that Douce gave him, and he plays with children his own age. He often asks for his mother, and Phébus, too, sometimes, but he never gives in to sorrow. My mistress regularly sends him asses' milk and white bread."

"Isn't he asked to show his scars to the passing pilgrims? Doesn't he suffer from being the son of a virgin anchoress?"

"The old woman has seen to that. She knows how to make people obey her. No stranger will ever find out that your child is in her house. As for the local people, they're used to him. There haven't been any miracles in the vicinity of your son, and he plays so much in the earth with the other kids that their palms all look alike. Nobody even notices him especially."

"And how he does he get to sleep without my hand? He always kept his fingers in mine, and couldn't sleep without them."

"He's been given a rabbit's foot and he's fine with that. He loves to snuggle up with the other brats on the straw mattress, and his arms and legs get all tangled up with theirs. The pilgrims, in the meantime, don't understand why you're refusing to see them. Some have even complained to Besançon about your lack of charity. The cathedral of Saint-Jean is protecting you, but the dean of the church of Saint-Étienne will eventually come all the way here to ask you the questions you fear, the ones nobody has dared ask you before now."

"Do you realize, Bérengère, that in trying to justify my reclusion I haven't even talked about my faith? Isn't it terrible to lose your direction like this in the middle of the journey, to no longer know either where you are going or how you will get home? To have no memory of why you set off in the first place? I condemned myself to wander until my death in a cell a few feet wide, and yet I've forgotten what I hoped to find within these walls."

"They won't let you wander in peace for long. Beware, your position is more perilous than you think! If you stay here, you have to play your role. Unless, of course, you can lie to those who come to tear off the halo the people around here have put on you. If you make up your mind to send me to Rome, Martin will escort me there."

God was still in my heart, but he had such a small place there now that I found it quite hard to pray calmly.

I chewed over my solitude in my cage, going around in endless circles, first in one direction, then in the other, until I was exhausted. Fourteen steps were enough to go all the way around. I had tried at first to push the walls away a little by reducing the length of my strides, but with all my privations I had ended up making myself so weak that this tiny walk had become a journey to the ends of the earth. My neglected body was beginning to stink, and what made my cell all the more stifling was that I now rarely opened my shutter. I had completely lost the strength my faith had given me all these years. My thoughts were no longer filled with prayer and contemplation, and now they tortured me. I had become an unbearable companion to myself, and time was stagnating.

I had loved my son as if he were Christ incarnate, and I had been exiled from the Child, the Host.

Had I finally lost all hope of beatitude?

It was then that I saw him, crouching in the shadows beside me. My heart leaped in my chest. He was watching me in silence, huddled in a corner. How had he been able to slip into my world without my noticing? How had he managed to enter that sealed tomb? He did not move, or hardly at all, and I avoided looking at his face for fear that it would drive him to stretch his legs and come toward me.

That terrible creature, Death or Devil, seemed endlessly reshaped, like silt being shifted, so much so that I could not make him my familiar. Even though I knew he was there, I gave a start each time my eyes fell on that dark form.

Had I invented him to struggle against my madness?

Had I projected the adversary outside me, in order to resist something other than myself? For there is nothing worse than a battle without an enemy.

I persuaded myself that if I fought him my child would soon return and run beneath the great maple.

So I retraced my steps and began praying nine times a day and opening my shutter to let the sun into my cell as soon as the bell rang for prime. I agreed to take food again (much to the joy of Ivette, who had grown as thin as me during that terrible period) and to wash myself. I even cut my hair and nails, had my tunic washed, and covered my head with a clear veil before declaring myself ready to receive the pilgrims, as well as poor Lothaire, who had been in despair over my madness. I kept going until that terrifying form had completely faded away. He was no doubt still there, somewhere in the room beside me or confined within my eyes, but I no longer feared him.

I had won my battle against death, now I just had to wait.

Elzéar would come back to me.

U nfortunately, my senses had been blunted, and neither the scent of roses, nor Bérengère's cries of pleasure, nor even Lothaire's songs had any effect on me now. I had lost joy and patience, and my visitors bored me. How predictable mankind was!

So, to make the time pass more quickly, I played with those unknown sinners, manhandled their souls. If I could not believe in God, I began to believe in myself, in the force of my words, whose incredible power seemed to grow with every passing day, and I used my position as I would never have dreamed of using it before. Even Douce again called me ambitious.

"I am a bowl into which men have poured their shadows," I told her, "and my glass sides have darkened with their sorrows. I've filled my heart with their sins, their fears, their misery, and now it is overflowing like a river in full spate. But they continue to feed the anchoress, they continue to throw their sins in the black water hoping to drown them there. Can't they see that the bowl is full? Can't they see that my heart is bursting and that my sorrow can no longer bear theirs? Douce, believe me, my only ambition is to survive until my child returns."

I had become more terrifying than a prophetess and I advised sinners to mortify their flesh.

The saint had grown bitter in her stone cask.

How I laughed at those penitents who obeyed me so will-

ingly and stood for days on end in my chapel, their arms out-
stretched in the shape of a cross, reciting verses of the Bible!
How I mocked those creatures who did exactly what they were
told when I enjoined them to spend one night lying naked with
a rotting corpse to make up for some offense done to a dead
person!

I was now so popular that the local people imposed silence
on those who complained of my severity. Malcontents were
told that a pilgrim from Cologne who had spoken badly of me
had suddenly found himself mute, his tongue stuck to his
palate. Death's abdication and the successive good harvests
since my entombment pleaded so well in my favor that nobody
in the region would have accepted my being dishonored.

My blessing had the force of a lucky charm, and people
demanded it. Little girls were called Esclarmonde so that they
could benefit from all my attention. A candle that I had
blessed was lighted whenever a new animal was born in a cow-
shed. I was credited with so many miraculous recoveries that
the local peasants prayed to me more than they prayed to most
of the saints recognized by the Church. And the more
demanding I was, the more touchy and unpredictable my
behavior, the more powerful I seemed to them. My whims and
follies increased tenfold the power of mercy that was attributed to me.

Occasionally, one of my visitors would distract me a little.
As a reward, I would invite him or her to pick a flower from
the rosebush Lothaire had planted almost four years earlier
outside my window and which he himself kept pruned. The
bush produced magnificent late roses, their red ever darker as
it aged, and I was associated with their scent. Those who left
with their flowers in their hands felt invincible. Martin would
pay me a visit every week with the sole purpose of receiving a
rose, which he then hastened to sell to the highest bidder.

When he was not sufficiently amusing for my taste, I would refuse him his reward. His crestfallen expression was irresistible.

I remember giving a rose to a very young woman who accused herself of having killed her husband. She was not a local girl, but, having heard about me, she had followed some pilgrims on their way to Rome with the sole purpose of meeting me and telling me her story.

"And how did you kill the poor man?" I asked her.

"I did as my confessor said."

"Your confessor?"

"My husband wasn't well. He was coughing a lot and wheezing rather than breathing. Everyone in our village knew how rough he was, he'd punish me for no reason, and several times left me for dead. That a man so full of vigor should feel so weak that he no longer beat me, that was what really got the neighbors thinking. So they told the priest. He's always looking at me in a funny way, that priest, always telling me I'm pretty. He sent for me to hear my confession and asked me all these questions he read out from his penitential, and as he did he went all red. It was one of those questions that gave me the idea of getting rid of my husband for good."

"Which one?"

"The priest asked me—I remember it exactly because I repeated those words endlessly on the way back home, to make sure I'd got it into my head—he asked me: 'Did you do what some wicked women do? Did you smear your naked body with honey, place corn on a cloth laid on the ground, did you roll around on it, carefully collect all the grains that had stuck to your body, then grind them, turning the millstone in the opposite direction from the sun, and make bread for your husband from the flour in the hope that he would waste away?'"

"Did you make that bread?"

"I didn't think it was too complicated, so I followed the

instructions to the letter. We had the corn and the beehives. I baked the bread and my husband passed away that night."

"So now you're free?"

"Not for long. My father's going to marry me off again soon. In any case, my husband didn't leave me anything, he had a son my age from his first marriage. I'm really glad I never gave him a child. He was a nasty piece of work."

"Don't you miss him?"

"Even though he left me with nothing, I'm calmer now that he's dead, but I'm really afraid of going to Hell. It isn't Christian to kill your fellow human being thanks to old formulas the priests are always fighting against, and it's even worse when you've slept with the victim and married him. Where I live, if they found out about all of that, I don't know what they'd do to me. I've come to see you because they say you don't gossip, and it's easier for me to confide in a girl. They say so many things about you, I just had to see you! So I walked all the way here with my great secret and now it's come out by itself. With the priest, it's much harder. Even trivial little sins stay in my mouth, I don't know what to say, and he has to look for his questions in his book. And besides, he is a man after all . . ."

"Then take a rose, my daughter!" I replied with a laugh. "It wasn't your fault your husband died. Your priest's formulas are worthless."

I no longer refused gifts from visitors, but I did not keep them, I gave them away to those most in need locally, as well as to the poor people passing through so that they could spread my renown on the road to Compostela. I sometimes imposed long fasts on fat merchants from Besançon in penitence for the crimes they came to confess to me as if I had been a priest. After a few shrewd calculations, they did what such burghers always did: they paid local people to fast in their place for several days and everyone was delighted to receive forgiveness or wages thanks to the anchoress.

God had abandoned me, and so had my son, and I did whatever I wished with people to distract myself a little while waiting for Elzéar, who was growing up far from me, to at last return.

And yet, in spite of these small amusements, time was still too slow. Intoxicated by my own omnipotence, I ended up threatening Ivette with Hell to force her to disobey her mother and give me back my child. In her simpleminded way, she had a boundless admiration for me, and my words made her weep so much that the old nurse came in person to lecture me.

Supported by two of her sons, her frail carcass came toward me, walking with very small steps.

How her strength had declined in a few months, since the time she had come early in the morning to demand my child!

Her sick, broken body, made stiff by the years, had a great deal of difficulty in freeing itself from the earth. Her feet could barely tear themselves from it, and she held her torso well forward in order not to be thrown off balance by the small movements she still managed to impose on her old bones. It was as if the earth and the air were joining forces to prevent her from advancing, and she was having to struggle against the elements: the sharp but still air of early winter was attacking her like a high wind, the grass turned into mud beneath her heavy feet, and time itself had accelerated around her to the point that her walk seemed motionless. The smallest stone became a slope against which she stumbled. The world was no longer that flexible substance in which it is good to move, the substance from which one draws pleasure. The world, once full of delight, had frozen with her inside it—she was trapped in it like an insect stuck in the wax of a candle.

What a lesson in dignity, that old woman's slow steps!

How I admired her painful efforts to keep going, that patient struggle she was waging against the weight of her inert body!

She was groping her way forward in a blurred universe, stopping often to try to gauge the number of steps that still separated us, to evaluate the effort to be made before reaching the dark mass of the chapel. I read her blindness in her blank eyes, and all she saw of me was my stone shell.

My sharp words proved to have no effect on that brave woman, and her words were like a slap, as was her blind gaze. In that milky mirror, I saw the person I had become. Seized with a fit of rage against the woman who had carried away my child, I flew into a fury of curses, vomiting my bile behind my bars, roaring like a caged beast.

"You're a burden to the world, so give up your place, you dirty bitch! Do you know why you've lived so long? It isn't because you're a hard worker, or because my sacrifice has muzzled death. No, it's because Lucifer has been waiting for you to make one false move to take you straight to Hell! Now that you've fallen into his trap, the devils will drag you by your feet to the fire where those who steal children burn for all eternity. Give me back my son and repent, you wicked woman!"

My hair disheveled, my eyes drained, I was foaming at the mouth like one possessed, and I was very lucky that only friends saw me like that. It was not the hour for the pilgrims and, feeling the crisis coming ever since the first warning signs, Bérengère had gone to spread her laughter and shake her green curves on the other side of the courtyard, in order to attract all the men of the Whispers to her. As for the women, they almost all knew what it is to lose a child, and they forced the younger ones to keep silent.

Once my body had been drained of all its rage, once my

pain had been spat out, I was choked with sobs and fell to the ground.

After that cry I do not know how long I stayed like that, huddled on the ground, weeping for my mistakes.

For several days, the pilgrims were sent away and Bérengère made me drink extracts of flowers and herbs of which she alone knew the secret, and which expelled all the bile and melancholy from my body.

That purge calmed me, and time passed smoothly enough without anything else tormenting me, not even the anguish of seeing the dean of Saint-Étienne appear at my window, nor the memory of that messenger whom Archbishop Thierry II had dispatched to the earldom after my father's revelation, that cleric who was walking in my direction bearing my fate in a sealed letter.

I plunged myself into the study of the sacred texts brought me by my dear brother Benoît. Nothing ever seemed to trouble him, and his constancy reassured me. He alone of my entourage had remained the same. Time had no hold over him. Nothing ever lined his skin, disturbed his features, or shook his faith. He went through life easily, untroubled by doubt or changes of mood, walking every day in the footsteps of the day before, never straying from the path he had laid out for himself once and for all. Whereas I had entered my cell as if boarding a ship, and had weathered storms, landed in unknown lands, hoped for so much and lost everything. How could one learn so much, change so much, suffer so much, age so much, in such a small space?

Lothaire often visited me with his vielle. I now had a better understanding of his sorrow, our two sufferings were similar and, in that communion of sentiments, his gentle love touched me more than I could say. He sang like a wind instrument.

What a difference between a cry and a song! A splendid transformation of pain, the song restores what the cry has torn asunder.

My heart warmed at the sound of his music, I felt it moving beneath my ribs. Our bodies were in harmony on either side of my bars, and whenever our eyes chanced to meet, it was a delightful sensation.

It was from Lothaire that I learned of the return of our respective brothers. Benjamin and Amey had at last left the Holy Land only to enter the fabulous world of his poems.

He often composed songs for me retracing their adventures. He would tell me how his brother, Amey de Montfaucon, had been mortally wounded trying to protect my brother from a band of brigands, a host of wood sprites, or a pack of wolves—in his mouth the details were constantly modified and his stories were not words pinned to a page, but kisses formed by his lips and launched into the air, as lively as little birds—and how Benjamin, who loved his savior, had managed to lead him moribund to the castle of his beloved Countess of Joux whom Amey wished to see again one last time before dying. Lothaire would sing to me of the tears shed by the beautiful Berthe, not over the tragic fate of her husband Amaury, who had died in battle on his mad horse, but over the wounds of that childhood friend, who had returned from Palestine for her. He would sing to me of the soft kiss she had placed on Amey's lips, which had brought him back to life.

Our brothers, then, had been living for two moons at Joux, their exploits haunted the songs of the minstrels, and neither of them was in a hurry to leave that marvelous universe of fables and lays and return to the fold. They were unaware how many dangers lurked in that magic land.

Every time Lothaire came to the Whispers, he would give me news of Amey and Berthe in music, glorifying the powers of love and the boundless joy of those who gave themselves up to it body and soul. Then he would either weep over the fate of separated sweethearts or mock rejected lovers and the ridiculous nature of his own sorrow.

One morning, there was a great noise in the courtyard of the Whispers: a young knight had just arrived at top speed, bearing sad tidings. The boy, who seemed quite genuine, introduced himself as a companion of Amey and Benjamin who had come back with them from the Crusade, and asked to speak with Douce as soon as possible.

He was led into the great hall where the lady received, surrounded by her dogs. There, this young man, who had not featured in any of the songs, threw himself at her feet, weeping, before launching into the strangest story imaginable.

According to him, although everyone thought him dead, Count Amaury de Joux had returned from the Crusade that very morning on his famous horse. Since the reunion of Berthe and Amey, life had been so sweet in his castle that one could enter it without hindrance. The young messenger with the big brown curls had himself halted his journey there longer than he should have, in order to take advantage of that wonderful harmony and savor it at the side of my brother Benjamin. The portcullis was no longer lowered, the guards let themselves be lulled by the songs of the minstrels, the dogs fell silent. The bells had not yet sounded for terce, and, in that tranquility, nobody had noticed the return of the count. Surprised by such negligence, he had left Gauvin in the courtyard and rushed unannounced up the dark staircase of the keep to his nuptial chamber, which had become the love nest of Berthe and Amey. There, he had surprised them in his bed, lying tenderly in one another's arms.

The whole castle had trembled.

His people thought at first that they were dealing with a

ghost, and, faced with that furious specter, Lothaire's brother had not even tried to defend himself. Amaury de Joux, still dressed in his coat of mail, all shiny with blue steel, had dragged the astonished young knight naked into the courtyard, and in front of the whole household had lifted his sword and brought it down again and again, opening Amey's flesh in all directions, before plunging his blade into his belly up to the hilt. He had then turned toward his desperate wife and given her a sound thrashing, but had stopped short of killing her, condemning her instead to finish her days in a tiny jail from where she would be able to gaze her fill on the gibbet where he had ordered the naked, bleeding body of her handsome lover to be hung. As a husband, did he not have full power over his adulterous wife?

"Knowing we could do nothing," continued the young man with the long lashes who had come to report the whole history to Douce and was still trembling from the horrors he had seen, "Benjamin and I decided to escape as soon as possible from the fortress. And to avenge Amey's death, your stepson resolved to seize Gauvin. The count's charger obeyed nobody but its master, it resisted Benjamin, forcing him to linger in the courtyard. My friend fought with the animal, trying to bend it to his will, quite determined to let it die beneath him if it did not yield to him. The foaming monster reared and even tried to bite its rider, whom it was carrying despite itself. I was already outside, waiting for them at the edge of the woods, when I saw them come galloping through the gate just as Amaury de Joux ordered the castle's portcullis to be closed in order to stop them. The sharp points of the bars cut them in half, without either of them seeming to care at all. Benjamin and Gauvin continued their mad ride and passed me, as if in a fairytale. Half-horse and half-man, a mixture of flesh and shadow, trying to control one another, rushing toward an absurd battle beyond their deaths. I followed that fearsome pair through the forest and reached the territory of the Whispers, where—I swear to you, my lady—I saw Gauvin drag Benjamin into the green waters of the Loue, not far from your mill, and disappear without a trace. I waited on the bank, but in vain, before coming up here to inform you. Now that everything has been said, let me withdraw, milady, I have a fine friend to mourn."

Douce found it hard to believe this extraordinary story, and yet, if the tale had an ounce of truth, if one part of Benjamin had indeed been able to escape by stealing that mad horse, the count would want to track him down, alive or dead, and his trail would lead him to the Whispers. The wooden fences would not long resist the assaults of such a powerful lord. Messengers had to be dispatched to her vassals, to the archbishopric and to Montfaucon to ask for their help.

But how to explain this miraculous story to her allies? Would it not be said of the mistress of the Whispers that she let herself be taken in by tales, that she believed herself threatened by visions and spells? That this merely proved how wrong it was to entrust a fiefdom to an innocent woman? And so Douce hesitated and, for fear of being discredited, merely ordered that the peasants be allowed into the courtyard of the castle in case Amaury tried to take revenge on them for the death of Gauvin.

But it was too late.

The count and his knights were already outside the precincts of the Whispers.

Having by now heard the whole story, I trembled for my son, who was still out there. I hoped that the old nurse would be able to get him to the woods to protect him from the slaughter Amaury would be sure to perpetrate on his serfs if the desire so took him.

Never before, in the more than three years since her husband had left, had Douce had to face the slightest aggression.

Wrapped in her long blue pelisse, she rode out on her palfrey to meet the madman who was threatening the castle, as yet unaware that her son Phébus had inherited it.

When he saw her bearing herself with courage and heard her ask him in an affable tone what he wanted, Amaury calmed down a little.

"Your stepson tried to steal my charger. Thief and horse were killed by my portcullis. But my men saw their specters run off together toward your lands."

"So you have come all this way from Joux in the hope of finding ghosts?" Douce asked in surprise.

"I have come to demand reparation."

"I imagine that, having already cut my stepson in half, it will be difficult for you to take any more revenge on him."

"My wife transformed my castle into a brothel, my companion in battle was crushed beneath iron bars thanks to a young upstart, and what was dearest to me in the world has been taken from me. So yes, milady, I am indeed in a mood to torture a ghost!"

"Benjamin's companion, who tried to stop him and is not to blame in this affair, claims to have seen the specter of your horse drag its rider into the waters of the Loue and drown him."

At that moment, Bérengère appeared at the top of one of the two little towers that framed the gate. She had urged all the females present to follow her and replace the guards, persuading them that the count would not dare attack a place held by women, that he would lose his honor if he behaved like the leader of a band of brigands.

"Knowing Gauvin," Amaury resumed, having raised small, black, mischievous eyes toward these unusual guards, "he will emerge again from the river and take a much harsher revenge on your family and your servants than I could. Take care, ladies, when you go down to the banks of the Loue and throw your pieces of linen into the rushing water, take care not to disturb his sleep. I shall now withdraw and leave you to his wicked ghost."

"Would you be good enough to give us back my stepson's body, so that we may bury him?"

"Milady, your stepson is in the Loue, so go there with all these girls and fish him out!"

As Amaury's troop turned and rode off after their master, Douce sighed with relief. She was far from suspecting what the count's words would provoke in her people.

The women of the castle, who had all heard Amaury's threats, were already trembling at the thought of encountering Gauvin's specter in the woods, and that fear would last for centuries.

When night fell, the land no longer belonged either to God or to men. At night, nightmares came to life and prowled around those who slept. Amulets, prayers, old rituals protected the houses from a host of terrible creatures that seized control of the woods. People prayed not to be devoured by werewolves or caught by invisible hands and dragged into subterranean caves, for infants not to be dragged away by monsters, goblins, and demons, and for death not to come and howl over our roofs. They feared the powers of the shades whose legends populated the country, and it took a lot of courage to venture alone, lantern in hand, into the forest after twilight. Whoever did so immediately seemed suspect: what was his affinity with the supernatural forces that swarmed in the darkness, to dare brave them in that way? The children were not the only ones to tremble. In the evening, the elders would tell terrible stories that dissuaded the boldest of young men from slipping into the woods to surprise Martin and Bérengère in the throes of passion. Rare were those brave peasants who were not afraid, not only of the shadows of night, but of what they concealed, what was hidden in them. They huddled within their walls, as if the night were a perilous voyage on which it was best to embark asleep, in order to avoid unpleasant encounters. It was important not to mingle with the people who inhabited an underworld where all the old beliefs demolished by the Church had taken refuge, and where evil deities had hidden themselves for centuries from divine eyes. A space where witches were free to cry out in joy.

Truly, there was already so much to fear in this land that we had no need of one more source of fright! Now Amaury de Joux, abandoning the specter of Gauvin on the banks of the Loue, had just invented a new one for them.

The phantom charger did not waste any time in emerging again from the riverbed to graze amid the graves and gallop through the countryside, its hooves thundering. Starting the very day after Benjamin's death, the monstrous horse was spotted in the four corners of the territory. Each man swore he had heard it or seen it running outside his door or window. It was believed at first that the dawn swept it away, that the light made it withdraw, exercising its power over it as over most infernal creatures, but very soon a shepherd said he had passed it in broad daylight beneath a storm, carrying off a poor unknown young man on its back at an infernal speed. Then the beast's misdeeds multiplied, to the extent that after only one moon they had lost count of its victims. This miraculous stallion, supernaturally white, would lie in wait for pilgrims on the roads and drown in the Loue all those who tried to mount it.

Death had returned to the land in the form of a horse.

Its victims, though, were never local people. It must be said that, knowing the whole story, the natives of the Whispers avoided crossing its path. Many were those who boasted that they had seen it on the road, advancing in the other direction, and passed it without even looking at it.

I had recovered my reason and finally accepted my son's departure. But Ivette had barely spoken to me since the time I had threatened her. She would bring me my water, my straw, and my bowl in silence, but kept her distance, as if I were going to bite her. I was quite calm now, though, and was waiting patiently for my trial to end.

As the poor girl had stopped giving me news of my son, I asked Bérengère to go to the old nurse's house every other day to see Elzéar. She would set off on the road, her hair hidden beneath the green bonnet she had taken to wearing constantly. She would leave laden with the kisses and words I entrusted to her, phrases I made her learn by heart so that she could recite them to my child.

It was she who informed me that my son would soon be brought back to the Whispers, that he had filled out considerably in a few months, and that he was growing faster since he had stopped breathing the tainted air of my cell. She described him to me as a vigorous child who was already holding himself well on the back of his old horse. "He'll be given back to you this last Friday of Carnival," she announced, trying to hold back her tears. A lock of hair escaped from her bonnet, even though she had carefully adjusted the latter. Tenderly, my fingers put it back in place beneath the cloth. Was it a play of the light, a reflection due to the premature spring, or did that lock really have an emerald-green tint? Even today, when I recall that scene, I cannot make up my mind. I remember thinking that Bérengère's hair had taken on the color of the Loue and that it was to conceal this strangeness that she kept it confined beneath a bonnet.

The world in my time was porous, easily penetrable by the miraculous. You have cut the connections and reduced the legends to nothing, denying what you have escaped, forgetting the power of the old stories. You have stifled magic, spirituality, and contemplation in the commotion of your cities, and there are few of you who take the time to listen carefully and still hear the music of old times or the sound of the wind in the branches. But don't go imagining that by destroying those tales you have chased away fear! No, you still tremble without even knowing why.

Thanks to the whims of the moon, Easter was late that year and spring seemed to have settled in even before the beginning of Lent. The maple was rich in foliage, and the sun filtered through its transparent young leaves. Elzéar would soon be four and I would see him again, I would be able to tell him of my love, touch him through the bars, and even kiss him if he climbed on the outer sill of my window. He would tell me of his life with the old woman, his great discoveries and all the wooden bridges thrown over the streams, he would show me the bow that Ivette's brother had made for him and which Bérengère had told me she had seen him using quite skillfully for such a little boy. As she could get to him so easily, I endlessly asked her to describe him to me, so that I could gain a clear idea of how he had grown and not appear too surprised when I saw him again.

We were still weeping for joy on either side of the bars of my cell when a cleric presented himself at the castle, a cleric whose thin figure I immediately recognized. It was he who had walked all the way from Acre to bring me his message. This envoy of fate had lost his way and taken a ridiculous length of time to reach the earldom of Burgundy and this castle of Whispers where Thierry II had sent him to bear his sealed message.

Why had he not died on the journey, this man who was about to subject me to the worst of trials just as my son was coming back to me?

When I saw him, I dried my tears of joy, and Bérengère immediately withdrew to make way for him, although, seeing from my expression that nothing good was likely to come of this visit, she preferred not to stray too far from my window.

After greeting me with a gesture, the cleric handed me the letter with the archbishop's red wax seal and waited in silence for me to break it. My trembling hands obeyed his eyes, and I found myself looking down at Thierry II's elegant handwriting.

My father had told him everything concerning Elzéar. As a penance for that lie of omission of which I had made myself guilty, he asked me to immediately take a vow of eternal silence. It was important, for both my son's good and that of the chapter of Saint-Jean, that I not say or write another word after receiving this letter. Thierry II added that the cleric facing me was mute, and that he would hear my last confession before my mouth was sealed forever, then he would take to Saint-Jean another letter in which it was specified that, if I refused to agree to that silence, my window would be walled up, leaving only a small crack high up in the wall, through which my food would be thrown to me until the day I died.

Aghast, I looked for a moment at the silent, impassive man facing me, and it struck me that it was no doubt his task to tear people's voices from them, that he harvested them far and wide, and that he amassed their secrets before sewing up their mouths.

How could I be thus mutilated? I had chosen reclusion, not silence. This time, the voluntary anchoress would become a genuine prisoner. I would no longer be just the captive of the fifteen-year-old who, imagining her happiness only in God, had asked for this chapel to be built, the innocent maid of the Whispers convinced that she could attain beatitude and freedom by walling herself up alive, an innocent who knew nothing yet of the world and had no idea how a person could change. No, by condemning me to silence and threatening to fill in my window, Thierry II was imposing an ordeal on me far greater than that poor foolish girl had ever imagined.

The man who had always condemned the burning of heretics at the stake was blowing on the embers of my funeral pyre from the afterlife.

And yet my mind could not bring itself to deny God. We

were living at a time when He was the driving force behind every one of his creations, when He was present in the smallest twig, when He watched over our every action. I could doubt men, my faith, and myself, but not His existence.

I obtained permission from the cleric to meditate for a moment before making confession and uttering my vow of eternal silence. Bérengère saw me close my shutter and, as the messenger had not withdrawn, she thought of the hagioscope.

She slipped into the chapel, stuck her mouth to the little hole that looked into my cell, and whispered to let me know she was there. I asked her to remain for a moment and quickly wrote the letter about which I had so often thought since that time when she had talked to me about knocking down the wall of my cell.

"Bérengère," I whispered, "I have very little time, so listen to me carefully. From now on, I am to be a prisoner of silence. You once offered to be my messenger. Now, before I utter my vow, I am entrusting you with this letter. Try to get it to the Pope. I know your power over men, you may well find a way to get through to him. Your chances are slim, and the road to Rome is a perilous one, but you are my one hope of getting out alive from these walls. What is asked of me today is beyond my strength. You have spoken so well on my behalf to my child lately, you will be able to find the words to tell Elzéar how much his mother loves him. I must be silent now on pain of never seeing him again and condemning myself to pray in darkness."

I affixed my seal to the rolled-up letter and slipped it into the hagioscope. Bérengère managed to get hold of it with the ends of her chubby fingers, and promised me that she would set off as soon as possible.

I opened my shutter and submitted to the will of an archbishop who had died crushed beneath his engine of war.

The cleric left for Besançon with my voice in his pouch.

*

My son returned to the Castle of Whispers two days later. Bérengère immediately brought him to me. How dark his skin and hair had become, how tall and handsome he seemed!

For a moment, my child stood dumbfounded outside my window, then ran off as fast as his legs would carry him, far from that terrible, mute, dirty, emaciated woman who was reaching out her arms to him through the bars and weeping.

Of course your age is no longer so quick to lock up young girls, but do not let that lead you to think that you are free of men's folly. I have seen the centuries pass, and History has never ceased to turn our lives upside down. The facts are infinitely mallcable.

Certainties are made of soft matter, they can easily be shaped as we wish.

As for death, what can I tell you about it except that since I died I have not achieved the lightness that would allow me, in escaping these stones, to reach the ether and perhaps see my son, and my mother, and Lothaire once again. For the dead, centuries are nothing. Time here does not resemble the time before death.

Now that the words have come out and there remains so little for me to say, it seems to me that the walls are beginning to relax their grip.

Fate was spreading its nets.

Bérengère thought she was offering me a way out by leaving for Rome. She announced her departure on the eve of the first Sunday of Lent, when fires were due to be lighted. I did not open my shutter to her and did not even hear her farewells.

When I entered my tomb at the age of seventeen, I had left nothing outside that I was not convinced I could sacrifice. My death to the world had not been painful, but sincere and joyous. But I was no longer that stubborn young girl so full of certainties. And now what had not existed at the moment I made my choice had been torn from me, the thing which, born with my reclusion, had taken all the space left vacant and replaced the forest, the wind, the vast sky, the strawberries in the woods, running barefoot in the grass, had even gained the upper hand over God's place and swept aside my plans by revealing me to myself. No, I was no longer the woman who had offered herself as a sacrifice, the woman who saw sainthood as the most wonderful of destinies and aspired to beatitude. And in that terrible void caused by the loss of my child, I had been condemned to silence, like some kind of purge. I was not being blamed for my ambition. It was not a heretic, a possessed woman, or a false prophet that was being gagged, it was a mother.

The children were making bundles of dead wood, laughing, preparing the straw torches that would be waved the following evening around the bonfires. Fires had always been lighted in the night on the first Sunday of Lent, and the whole cliff was lit up. It was one of those dates when the entire community took possession of the darkness and chased out the devils.

All the parts of the mechanism were in place, and all that remained was to let go of the rope, stretched by now to breaking point, in order for fate to fly like an arrow to its target.

To say that I heard the world's hubbub the day that Bérengère left would be a lie. I had withdrawn into myself. I was surrounded by my thoughts, I was a recluse within my own sadness, there were no more windows in the space into which my soul had retreated, just an endlessly repeated pain.

I only reconstructed the events later, when I had time to put them into some kind of order. I understood what had happened by looking at the living and listening to their prayers.

Bérengère was speaking loudly against my shutter so that I could hear her message from the depths of my sorrow.

"I swear to you, Esclarmonde, that I will do all in my power to free you from these stones. Your letter will be given to the Pope. Martin and I will do everything we can to make sure it is. I believe in love now. It has given me the confidence to set off through the world. I'm accused of being a witch and of casting spells on men. Well, the people here have seen nothing yet of my spells! You won't remain locked up, you'll leave these walls and live in the open air. Lothaire and your son are waiting for you outside."

Bérengère was almost yelling, taking no heed of Ivette, who was within earshot. She put all her strength of conviction in her voice to urge me to believe that there was indeed a way out. I heard nothing, but Ivette had no doubt that that cursed woman, that half-witch, would be able to get me out of my hole.

As the guards watched the huge green figure of Bérengère striding away from the Castle of Whispers and mourned the object of their desire, Ivette hurried to report the news. She ran to the first gossip she could find, the latter took over, and very soon the men were downing their tools, the women were abandoning their animals and their distaffs, and everyone was running from house to house, from field to field. The shepherds cried in the hills in their mysterious language and the echo of their cries spread though the region. Bérengère had not yet even crossed the Loue before the whole country already knew where she was going with her long strides.

Ivette continued to rush about in a panic, while the poor people gathered together, terrified by the words she had helped on their way across the countryside. They wept at the thought that Esclarmonde, the saint, was seeking to abandon her people, and that Bérengère, that foul witch, was setting off on the road to Rome to implore the Pope to free their anchoress.

Could their saint really be taken away from them? Where would she go to preach once she was free?

They all remembered how life had been before Esclarmonde had chosen to sacrifice herself for her people by shutting herself away and Death had decamped. The famines, the epidemics, the attacks from their neighbors, the tyrannical Lord of the Whispers, and even young Lothaire, now a gentle poet, who used to violate girls in the ditches: they all remembered that daily misery.

But now the land was yielding so much that even the serfs were growing fat. Above all, they no longer feared Death, whom the saint had chased away. It was not possible that the country could let its benefactress be stolen away by that big girl whose beauty was so unnatural, by that Bérengère and her accomplice in wickedness, that seller of false relics who had shaved the heads of so many local women to pass off their hair as the locks of Saint Agnes.

And simpleminded Ivette was still running around, recruiting bands of brats, unaware what the adults were plotting.

No, that demonic couple could not be allowed to persuade their saint to return to the world. It was essential that Esclarmonde remain at the Whispers, that she die there, and that her holy relics continue to protect this land beyond her death.

What would become of them if the anchoress went back on her word?

Fate was tightening its net.

The old nurse, who could no longer see a thing, was calling to her children without realizing that they had all suddenly left without saying anything to her.

Lothaire was riding toward me in the company of the minstrel who had taught him poetry.

A white charger was peacefully grazing on the gladioli in

the castle's ornamental garden, where maidservants and
guards, distracted from their tasks by the noise, had abandoned Phébus and Elzéar.

Bérengère and Martin were walking hand-in-hand beside
the Loue, while a crowd of hard-faced peasants, armed with
pitchforks, sticks, and sickles, was running to catch up with
them, and Ivette, the angriest of all, the most revolted at the
thought that I might abandon my task, was coming back
toward the chapel with all the children she had been able to
find on the way, a pack of excited youngsters, their arms laden
with sticks of wood and firebrands, which they had prepared
for the next day's feast. One of the youngest had already set
fire to his, and was laughing and running to catch up with the
others, waving his torch and spreading stars in the air.

All I saw was thick smoke coming in through the hagioscope and the cracks in my shutter and making my eyes smart.
The wooden framework of my chapel was in flames, transformed into a funeral pyre.

I had always thought that only heretics and criminals were
burned, and feared the judgment of the clerics or the provosts,
never that of the simple people who loved me so much. I had
no idea that they too, blinded by terror, sometimes committed
murders to stop a saint leaving his territory. I should have realized that my presence had turned into a real treasure and that
a saint's body kept all its powers even when that saint was
dead.

Bérengère and Martin were surrounded on the banks of the
Loue at a place where the willows grew close together and the
waters of the river ran loudly. Martin abandoned his donkey
and seized his club to protect Bérengère, who had slipped
behind him. Although neither was local, they knew a fair number of their pursuers and tried to understand what these peo-

ple wanted of them, these people who seemed to have gone mad, this mass of bulging eyes and faces reddened by running, this serried crowd approaching them slowly, pitchforks raised, and forcing them little by little into the deep, fast-running waters of the Loue, swollen by the spring thaw. None of these possessed people opened their mouths to answer their questions. Seeing that nothing could mollify them and that this stubborn crowd would not leave them without a battle, Martin advanced toward them, shaking his club to frighten them away. The pitchforks immediately stopped him, and the blows he received made him groan and fall into the water. Wounded in the chest, he tried to get back on his feet, but the current was too strong. Bérengère rushed to his rescue. They embraced, the water already above their waists, but the others continued pushing them without a word toward deeper waters. The group had decided that they must die, and my friends sensed that there was nothing to be done, that these good people, impervious to anything but their own rage, were hungry for blood. Then Bérengère smiled at Martin, they looked at each other with a tenderness that wiped away their fear, and, in a last kiss, they abandoned themselves to the raging waters of the Loue.

It has long been said that just as the river was about to swallow the couple, Bérengère's bonnet had slipped off, freeing a wave of hair as green as seaweed.

After this tragedy, the peasants retraced their steps, knowing already that Bérengère would not let go of them and that her strange beauty would haunt them until their last breath.

The country forgot her story and her name, but she changed into a figure that still haunts the banks of the Loue— she became the one now called the Green Lady, who, like a mermaid, seduces men, enjoys their bodies, cries out in the night, then, sated, draws then into the waters and drowns them, smiling that same smile of passionate love that Bérengère had on her face when she died in the arms of her fat Martin.

*

In the castle's ornamental garden, the horse continued to graze, while Phébus and Elzéar watched it in awe. It was such a handsome beast and seemed so tranquil that the two children stroked it and ended up leading it, laughing, to a tree stump, which they used to climb on its back. The horse did not react. It was only when it smelled the fire and heard Douce's screams from the window of her bedchamber that it raised its head, rolled its eyes in fright, and set off at a gallop toward the great door. The children fell off immediately. Elzéar rolled in the grass, but Phébus broke his neck on a stone. Douce, who had come running into the garden, ignored everything else—the fire in the chapel, the horse, Elzéar. Weeping, she carried her unconscious son to his bed and tried in vain to revive him. The child's heart beat for a few more hours without giving any other sign of life than a distant noise of horses' hooves in his chest.

The horse was never seen again, and the scatterbrained maidservants, who had gone with the peasants to hunt down Bérengère, added Phébus to the long list of victims of the specter of Gauvin. Not that it was their fault if Benjamin had stolen that mad beast and led it to Hell. The child would have succumbed one day or another to the horse's rancor. You could not fight a curse.

Just before entering the courtyard of the Castle of Whispers, Lothaire met a flock of peasant children all running in the same direction and chirping like starlings, then, having passed through the studded oak gate, he suddenly saw a magnificent riderless white charger galloping with its belly close to the ground. He was unable to bar its way, and was surprised that those children had been running from such a fine horse. The ghost of Gauvin, of which he sang so much in his lays, came back into his head and he smiled, thinking of the strength of tales.

He was about to set off in pursuit of the animal when he saw the smoke. Abandoning his previous thoughts, he immediately set off full tilt for my chapel, the roof of which was already in flames.

Knowing he would be unable to control the fire that was devouring the roof timbers, he merely stamped on the pyre that had been lit before my window, while his companion the minstrel ran to look for a sledgehammer. He then kicked down what remained of my shutter, looked in, and saw me lying motionless in my tomb. The bars were set so deeply in the stone that nobody would have been able to tear them out. The two men therefore took turns in the burning nave knocking down with the sledgehammer the least solid of the walls enclosing me—those bricks that had been placed before the door of my cell five years earlier.

Lothaire and his friend beat on the side of Sainte-Agnès beneath a shower of red-hot sparks falling like stars from the glowing sky. They struck the brickwork, surrounded by the thick, acrid smoke spat out by the fire. Groping, they cleared the layer of stone, and then, their eyes burned by the heat of the inferno, attacked the wood of the door. Thanks to the strength of their blows, my tomb opened. The fire roared, the beams cracked. Lothaire managed to extricate me from my cell just before the roof of the building collapsed.

Out of breath, he placed my lifeless body beneath that maple that had loyally offered me its colors and scent through the years. The wind was blowing the smoke in the other direction, and nothing blurred the lacquered blue of the sky above my tree.

I remember struggling for a moment to open my eyes, so luminous was the world.

How dazzling everything was!

The sun was playing in the foliage and the still-transparent leaves of the great tree. These last images have carved themselves into my soul for all eternity.

I remember feeling the air on my skin, the grass between my fingers, and my tongue tied by my promise,

I remember the voice of Elzéar in the distance calling his brother Phébus,

I remember Lothaire's warm lips and his breath on my mouth trying, as in a fairy tale, to bring me back to life,

But I knew that, in spite of that kiss, I was dying.

I remember that I seemed to hear the bell of Sainte-Agnès ring one last time, and I wished I could wait to see how long the sound would vibrate in the air . . .

I left in love with the vast sky contained in Lothaire's gentle eyes.

After my end, Death, as if driven wild, swooped down on the fiefdom.

My old nurse was the first to be carried off. She died alone, sitting on the threshold of her cottage where she had dragged herself to watch with her blank eyes for the return of her children, who had set off along the banks of the Loue without a word to her.

Little Phébus followed her the very next day. And then the Grim Reaper, made hungry by five years of fasting, seized a whole stream of young people, many of whom had started to think of themselves as immortal and to behave accordingly. The ashes of Sainte-Agnès were collected in little casks, and people prayed to me morning, noon, and night and threw offerings into the Loue, but nothing worked. Death had taken his place again.

They were angry at themselves for having gone so mad on that day before the first Sunday in Lent, when, for the first time, no fire had burned in the night. Only the river had glowed in the moonlight, with a strange green glimmer. That day of collective madness had made such a strong impression that nobody said a word when Douce changed Elzéar's name to Phébus and raised him as her son. Nobody said a word, and Douce was able to stay at the Whispers without any of her brothers trying to marry her off again. It was she who had Sainte-Agnès rebuilt exactly as it had been, and placed my corpse in a reliquary inside it.

Not a day went by without her coming to ask my forgiveness for having stolen my child after my death.

Having become Lord of the Whispers, my son often stopped in the spot where my cell had once stood. He felt a connection to these walls, and did not understand the nostalgia that caught him by the throat as soon as he approached the patch of ground where he was unaware he had lived beside me. Of course, he knew that a woman had been walled up here, in this place where a magnificent rosebush grew covered in dark flowers, but nobody at the Whispers spoke any longer of Esclarmonde and nobody would have dared remember that the anchoress was his mother. Only the woman named Ivette with her ruined smile, her mind drifting, would mutter things to him in a language that nobody understood, and her eyes would light up like coals as she held my son's pierced hands in hers.

Until the day he died, my child probed the stone with his eyes in search of an answer.

We pass the spot where the huge gate of oak and iron once stood, and tread the tall grass of the fallow grounds that stretch before the north face of the castle.

The wind sweeps shadows over the great tower and its wings. The daydream that ruffled the stone façade of the castle lifts like mist.

A man lives here sometimes, but he is not here at the moment, he works in Paris. It is said he has pierced hands.

The locals call the route we took to get up here the Path of the Witch.

It seems to us as if a horse is galloping not far away. We can hear the noise of its hooves beating on the stones.

On our right, a few gravestones are scattered in unsettled disorder outside a very old chapel.

We half open the door of the building and slip inside. The stained glass windows are all broken, and the winds pass through like the breath in a flute.

On one of the walls, we manage to decipher this almost obliterated inscription:

In this year 1187, Esclarmonde, Damsel of the Whispers, resolves to live as an anchoress at Hautepierre, confined until her death to the little sealed cell built for her by her father against the walls of the chapel that he erected on his lands in honor of Saint Agnes, who was martyred at the age of thirteen for having accepted no other bridegroom than Christ.

A bell rings in the valley of the Loue and we wait for its last peal to see how long the echo lasts.

ACKNOWLEDGMENTS

The author would like to thank the Department of Seine-Saint-Denis for its support, within the framework of the *Écrivains en Seine-Saint-Denis* program.

ABOUT THE AUTHOR

Carole Martinez teaches French at a middle school in Issy-les-Moulineaux. She began writing during her maternity leave in 2005. *The Castle of Whispers* is her second novel.